Rough Stock

Rough Stock

Heather B. Moore
Rebecca Connolly
Sophia Summers

Mirror Press

Copyright © 2021 by Heather B. Moore

Print edition

All rights reserved

No part of this book may be reproduced in any form whatsoever without prior written permission of the publisher, except in the case of brief passages embodied in critical reviews and articles. This is a work of fiction. The characters, names, incidents, places, and dialog are products of the author's imagination and are not to be construed as real.

Interior design by Cora Johnson

Edited by Joanne Lui, Lorie Humpherys, and Laramee Fox

Cover design by Rachael Anderson

Cover image credit: Period Images

Published by Mirror Press, LLC

ISBN: 978-1-952611-14-8

Lost Creek Rodeo Series

Round Up

Chute Boss

Rough Stock

Full Rigged

Half Hitch

Ace High

NOTE TO READERS:

All characters and situations in this book are fictitious and do not represent actual people or situations.

The following towns and locations in this series are also fictitious:

Lost Creek
Sam Houston Community College
Broken Hearts Ranch
Prosper
Mount Palmer

CHAPTER 1

SILVIA DIAZ KICKED OFF her stilettos and closed her eyes. Thankfully, the lights had dimmed at the charity auction, and no one could see her. And her feet were under the table, so they stayed hidden.

Her brother, Axel Diaz, was the keynote speaker tonight. As well he should be. He'd been on the board of the Sports for Kids charity for years, and if that alone wasn't impressive, how about his stellar career as Major League Baseball's top shortstop? His playing for the pro baseball team the Seattle Sharks had brought Silvia and her mom to Seattle when she was a teenager.

Now, at the age of twenty-four, she was so over it.

Over all of this.

She knew she should be grateful. And she was.

She knew she should be proud of her brother. And she was.

She knew she should count her blessings about her mother's near cancer scare last month that had turned out to be benign. And she did.

But . . . Silvia had been living in her brother's shadow

forever. At least, it seemed so. Ever since he started playing baseball, she and her mom had gone to most of his games. To support *him*. No matter what Silvia had going on, everything was dropped when her brother had a game. He'd then turned his success into supporting their family, which put him even more into the father role in her life.

Maybe if her dad hadn't left when she was two years old, then this all wouldn't have happened, and her brother wouldn't be acting like her dad all the time. Her parents could have been their son's number one support, and Silvia could have lived her own life, made a few decisions on her own, scooted a bit farther from the spotlight.

The audience began to clap, and Silvia realized she hadn't been listening to a word her brother had said. She focused on him now. His dark hair gleamed beneath the bright lights of the stage. His body, which was in top physical condition, seemed made for the tuxedo he wore. His olive skin set off the white flash of his teeth and his dark brown eyes—which mirrored hers.

His words were eloquent and heartfelt, and the audience was eating them up.

Silvia had no doubt tonight would be a record-breaking fundraising night for Sports for Kids. The charity raised money for underprivileged kids who wanted to play sports, but their parents couldn't afford it. Sports for Kids paid for team and uniform fees.

"You might think I'm here because I'm looking for a tax write-off," Axel told the audience.

A few chuckled. Everyone knew very well that wasn't the case.

"But the truth is, I was one of these kids."

Silvia had heard Axel's speech many times. She didn't remember her dad, and it used to bother her that Axel was so open about their family problems, but now, she felt numb to it. She'd stopped caring. Mostly.

"My dad's alcoholism turned him into a man no longer fit to be a father and husband," Axel said. "When he left my mom, me, and my baby sister, he took everything. The only reason I'm standing here today is because of the compassion, and the open wallet, of a Little League coach in Southern California."

The room erupted into clapping, and most of the audience wiped at tears in their eyes.

All right. So Silvia was moved as well. Who wouldn't be when hearing stories of her brother and these kids—kids who didn't always have enough to eat, either. She blinked back a stray tear before it fell on her cheek, then felt a pat on her shoulder.

She looked over at Brighton, Axel's wife. Her dark hair was swept into an elegant twist. Brighton smiled at her with sympathy, and Silvia smiled back. But inside, she was annoyed. She didn't want sympathetic looks or smiles. She didn't always want to be known as Axel Diaz's baby sister. Silvia wanted to be taken seriously. She'd finally gotten up the courage to tell her brother that she was dropping out of college—which he was paying for—because she wanted to go to hair school instead.

Or not. Truthfully, she didn't know. But staying one more week at the community college wasn't an option. She'd already dropped her classes—though Axel didn't know that. Being surrounded by eager students who discussed test and quiz scores like they were debating a presidential candidate was so far out of Silvia's interest that she'd begun to develop anxiety about going to class. Not the normal stress of any other college student, but anxiety so crippling that some days, she stayed in her dorm all day.

Fortunately, she had her own private bedroom, and her roommates didn't much care if she was coming or going. They were caught up in their dating drama.

Speaking of dating . . .

Silvia slipped her phone out of her clutch to see that Darren had texted a few minutes ago. She hid a smile, since Axel was talking about how a twelve-year-old girl had gotten out of a bad home situation, and now played on a top club basketball team. It would look rude to be smiling during that story.

Hey babe, I got off work early. Can you meet up?

Her pulse thrummed at the invitation. Darren had finally started paying attention to her. He'd dated one of her roommates a few weeks back, but things were over between them now. Still, they had to keep their relationship on the down low.

I'm at a charity thing with my brother, and he's my ride.

The three dots on the text app danced for a few seconds.

Need a getaway car?

Her heart slammed into her chest. Should she? Did she dare?

I'd love one.

Send me a pin, babe.

She sent the pin just as she heard her brother say, "And one of our volunteers at the office is here tonight. My sister. Silvia, will you come up and say a few words?"

Heads turned, necks craned, and people started to clap.

Silvia felt her heart drop to her stomach. Yeah, she volunteered once a week at Sports for Kids, but so did a lot of people. Axel had not warned her about this, and he knew how much she hated the limelight.

With trembling hands and an ultra-fake smile, she slipped her phone into her clutch. The last thing she wanted was for Brighton to see any texts from Darren. Another sore point with her brother and his wife. They were both freaks about who she did and did not date. Just because Axel had been known as "Cold Axe" before he met Brighton didn't mean Silvia had to stay home on the weekends.

The clapping increased, and Axel was waiting for her, his winning smile somehow not making her feel any better.

Silvia couldn't very well pause to put on her shoes—everyone was watching her now. Hundreds of eyes. Well, maybe two hundred pairs. But that was a lot. Really, a lot.

Brighton nudged her. "They're waiting for you, Silv."

Silvia swallowed, her throat feeling like the Sahara Desert. They *were* waiting for her. And they were still looking at her. Clapping. Smiling.

Her gaze connected with another man across the table. Grizz. One of Axel's best friends and former teammate at Belltown. Grizz was currently the all-time best catcher in the MLB, and his wife Rachel was next to him, all smiles. She'd been one of the top dancers in Chicago, and now she had her own studio, in addition to an adorable brood of three kids. No losers at this table. Except for maybe Silvia herself.

But Grizz wasn't smiling. His gaze was intent on her, his brow furrowed, his expression . . . concerned.

Could he tell she was about to have a panic attack?

No, no one could tell, because she wasn't going to have one. She was going to walk to the stage like a normal person, deliver a dazzling speech about how her life had been changed through her volunteer work, then escape with Darren for a fun, irresponsible night doing what twenty-something college dropouts did . . .

But she never made it to the stage.

Silvia stood and took a handful of steps before her legs turned to water. And her breath rushed out. Then the room spun.

Her last memory was of Grizz McCarthy's deep voice as his arms circled her. "Someone call 911."

Chapter 2

THE PRO RODEO CIRCUIT was taking Westin Farr within spitting distance of Lost Creek, and he was more thrilled than a kid getting a bike for his birthday. He grinned at the rodeo event schedule on his beat-up phone as a baseball game played in the background of the truck stop he'd pulled into. A quick shower, some toothpaste against his pearly whites, and he was good to go for another day.

He glanced up at the television as the baseball crowd cheered for a double-base hit. The runner on third didn't make it home. No. Not with Grizz McCarthy on the home bag. Not much got through that beast of a man. Westin might be a rodeo man, but he always respected those who took their sport seriously. Grizz was one of those guys.

As the next batter stepped up to the plate, Westin returned to the event schedule on his phone. Last night, he'd ridden Spitfire at a northern Texas rodeo. He'd lasted the eight seconds and earned the first-place purse. Not too shabby.

There hadn't been time to celebrate the win. Or his birthday. He had another rodeo to get to. Besides, he never celebrated his birthday anymore, because it was also the anniversary of his dad's death. And frankly, Westin's dad had been everything to him. Bud Farr had been a rodeo legend in his own right, only the second cowboy to score a 100-point bull ride in history. Wade Leslie had been the first. And Westin planned to be the third. In honor of his dad's memory, of course.

At the age of twenty-eight, Westin might be on the older end of the spectrum as far as bull riders went, but he'd been a late bloomer in everything, including attending Sam Houston Community College, the agricultural college in a small Texas town that utilized the Lost Creek rodeo arena for the college rodeo team. A group Westin had been able to open up to. The guys shared his grief about his dad. Heck, they'd all idolized him, and now his former college buddies were all well into their own rodeo careers. The Original Six, they were called by some.

And in just a few hours, Westin would be rolling into Lost Creek again—a town with so many good memories. He couldn't wait. The riders weren't all confirmed, but he was hoping that more than just Ford and Eric would be there. Ford was a hockey player turned rodeo star. They never tired of razzing him about that. And Eric, a good ole Wyoming kid, was the salt of the earth. Ryan Prosper would also be there; he was local to Lost Creek. In fact, his sister, Kellie, had turned part of their family ranch into some sort of women's recovery center. Ryan wouldn't be entering any rodeo events because of a career-ending injury, so now he was the designated host for anything in Lost Creek.

A text buzzed on Westin's phone, and he opened the group app where the Lost Creek boys posted their latest and greatest news. Or sometimes just ribbed each other. They called their group text "The Chute." Fitting.

Who's in the house tonight? Lars had written. He was

even older than Westin, and Lars always made a point to complain about the Texas heat, being a Montana boy.

You coming to Lost Creek, Montana? Ford wrote back immediately.

Lars: *What if I am? You got dinner arranged?*

Ryan's cooking for us all, Ford said.

Ryan: *What???*

Westin laughed. This was too good to miss. Another crowd roar sounded from the television in the corner of the truck stop café, and Westin slid out of the booth where he'd eaten a heated egg and sausage sandwich. All in all, it had been a decent stop. Westin never bothered with hotels since it was a hassle to check in and out, not to mention tough on the old wallet. He dumped his wrappers in the trash, then headed outside to his truck, reading texts as he went.

Your town, you cook, Ford continued.

Ryan: *Sure, whatever. How many of you yahoos are coming tonight? You probably heard that Knox Prosper is riding the bulls—and he's Westin's number one competition. Can't let a good event go to waste. West? You on your way? Heard about the win last night. Congrats, man. You're going to give Knox a good run.*

On my way, and thanks, Westin typed.

If Lars is coming, then we only need Reid, and it will be epic, Eric wrote.

Eric, baby, you finally opened your baby blues and joined the rest of the civilized world? Lars wrote.

Eric: *Been up since five, even though I'm no longer milking cows. Can't seem to shake the habit.*

A series of laughing emojis followed, plus one with a mooing cow.

Ford: *Reid. Stop watching the grass grow. You coming to Lost Creek?*

Reid: *Don't know. Can't think with all these texts blowing up my phone.*

Time's up. You in or you out? Ford could be persistent, to say the least.

Westin started up Bessy—his truck. She was over the hill, but he wouldn't part with her for anything. Her cherry red color and immaculate interior were his pride.

Reid: *I'm in. But I expect a clean bed and three meals a day.*

Ford: *Ryan's on it.*

Lars sent a series of GIFs of various forms of celebrating dogs, cats, and even a chimpanzee wearing a party hat as he blew into a striped party horn.

Westin laughed to himself, then set the phone aside as he pulled away from the truck stop. The phone continued to chime, but he turned up the volume on the radio station, drumming his fingers on the steering wheel in time to the country music. It would be good to see the guys again. Good for his soul.

And he couldn't wait to compete with Knox Prosper head on. Knox was Ryan and Kellie's cousin. The guy had gone off the grid for a while. Messed up his marriage, began to party, got kicked out of a few rodeo events. But the past few months, he'd been tearing up the circuit. Posting top scores and winning big purses.

No matter. Westin could take him. He turned the music up a notch, completely drowning out the sounds of his phone. The Texas sky was a bright blue today, and he was expecting hot temperatures even though it was only May. One thing Westin learned from being born and raised in Oklahoma was to appreciate every state he visited. To find something he loved.

Hands down, in Texas, it was the Tex-Mex food and the wide open sky that seemed to go on forever.

The drive ahead was several hours, but he didn't mind.

Westin wasn't a guy who had to be entertained. Give him a truck, a wide open road, and some good music, and he considered that as good as it got.

When the music changed on the radio station, Westin realized his phone was ringing. He never answered when he was driving since he didn't have one of those fancy Bluetooth things, and his truck was way too ancient to have any sort of synced up system.

But if it was his mom calling, he'd pull over and call her back. He didn't like her living alone, but she insisted, even after an invitation from his younger sister to move in with her. It wasn't that his mom couldn't take care of herself—she could do that, definitely. But the ranch was way too much for her.

Yes, they had ranch hands, and the like, but the house itself was hard to keep up for one person. Westin's one and only sibling lived about one hundred miles away from their childhood home. She'd married a hotshot lawyer, and they'd moved to the city. They had a little boy, Jeppsen, who was three now, and another kid on the way.

Sure, Cheryl was good about checking up on their mom, but she was still one hundred miles away.

But the caller ID on his phone didn't flash "Mom" across the screen. Instead, it had illuminated with a name he should have deleted from his phone months ago. Amy. His ex-girlfriend, and for a good reason, too.

It wasn't every guy, or any guy, in the world who'd put up with her antics and stay together. He hoped she was getting help, but he doubted it. Amy didn't see anything wrong with her obsessive ways—about him—and the fact that she acted erratically sometimes. Which led him to believe she was abusing substances.

But when he'd confronted her, she'd denied it. Just told

him she had a cigarette once in a while. The weeks and months had passed, and he'd seen the pills when she'd dropped her purse and some things spilled out. They weren't prescribed to her. Again, she covered up with lies.

Lies that Westin was no longer interested in putting up with.

The phone stopped ringing, and Westin wondered if she'd leave a message.

Nothing came.

He was just starting to relax into the tunes from the radio again when his phone rang again. Amy.

Westin's gut clenched, and he knew if he didn't talk to Amy, she'd stay on his mind. And it would be torture.

She'd been fun and easygoing when they'd first met at a rodeo near his hometown. Amy had said she was from Oklahoma, too—something he discovered was a lie later. He'd asked her out—because frankly, she was beautiful and sweet and charming. It was on their third date that he noticed something off. She drilled him with questions that were intrusive. Acted jealous and possessive, to the extreme. Then she waited at his mom's house for him to come home when he was on his way back from out of town.

The day he found her inside his house, waiting, was the day he knew he had to end things. His mom wasn't around, and Amy had let herself in. She simply didn't respect boundaries, and it didn't help that she was also calling and texting at all hours of the day. Westin was a nice guy, but not that nice.

When he'd broken things off, she'd thrown a fit, of course, and threatened never to talk to him again. Which was fine with him.

So why was she calling now? After so much time?

He exhaled as he pulled over to the side of the road, then he answered the call.

"Amy?" he said into the phone. "What's going on?"

"Westin," her voice purred. "How are you?"

He closed his eyes. "Why are you calling?"

She exhaled, and he could see her pout in his mind. Not his favorite image.

"I'm in your neighborhood, sugar," she said. "Thought we could meet up. You know, talk about old times."

"I'm out of town." He had to be direct, even blunt with her. Because he knew from experience that if he gave an inch, she'd take ten miles. "Even if I were in town, we wouldn't be meeting. Our relationship has been over for months."

"Just because we're not dating, it doesn't mean we can't be friends."

Westin gritted his teeth for a moment. "I'm sorry, Amy. It does mean we aren't friends. I thought we talked about this before. There's no future *anything*—"

"You think you're all that, don't you, Westin Farr?" Amy cut in. "Well, I'm here to tell you that you're one big poser. You'll never—"

He hung up before she got too far into her rant. Not that he was surprised. It only confirmed his original decision. Then he blocked her number. Next, he called his mom. Told her about Amy's call.

"Sorry she's still bothering you," his mom said. "Don't worry about me. I'll keep everything locked up."

This only brought a small amount of relief to him, so he called his sister, Cheryl.

"She's nuts," his sister said. "You might want to file a restraining order after all."

Westin didn't think things needed to go that far. "I'll hold off on that. I just wanted you to know because mom's alone."

"I'll see if she wants to come here for a few days, and I'll start following Amy on social media again if you want," Cheryl said. "Track what she's doing for a bit."

If there was one thing Amy lived and died by, it was Twitter. She narrated her entire life on that platform. In fact, she was probably throwing him under the bus right now. Ranting about their phone call.

"Okay, thanks," Westin said. "Let me know if there's anything I need to be aware of."

"Will do. Love you, baby brother."

"You'll never stop calling me that, will you?"

Cheryl laughed. "You'll always be my little brother, so no."

Westin shook his head, but he was smiling.

When they hung up, he had a warm spot in the center of his chest. He knew he was lucky to have such a great relationship with his mom and sister. Not all of his buddies had that.

The next hour of driving was uneventful, thankfully, and by the time he neared the town of Lost Creek, he was good and hungry again. He slowed to turn off the highway and headed to the first gas station. His truck was nearly empty, and he should probably fill up now so he wouldn't have to worry about it.

As he turned onto the exit, he was surprised to see a young woman walking alongside the road, her thumb out.

It wasn't that hitchhikers were completely unusual, especially in more rural settings, but this woman looked as if she were fiery mad . . . if the way she was dragging a suitcase, with its one wheel, behind her was any indication.

Westin felt a bit sorry for her suitcase.

And the woman? She was a petite, curvy woman, hair black and streaming behind her with the help of the wind, and she wore a t-shirt that said *Sharks*, along with shorts that gave him a good view of her legs.

Eyes on the road, he told himself.

But his gaze strayed again.

He wasn't in the habit of picking up hitchhikers. Besides, this woman looked like trouble. He didn't need any more trouble in that department.

Also, she was walking the opposite direction that he was heading.

What if . . . what if some creep picked her up?

Westin grumbled at his intruding thoughts. She was an adult woman, and she was making her own choices. Right?

He passed her, keeping his jaw locked, gaze straight ahead, but then his eyes shifted to his rearview mirror. She nearly stumbled.

Oh, had he mentioned she was wearing high heels with those short shorts of hers?

Definitely trouble.

With a sigh and another regret to add to his list, Westin turned his truck around.

CHAPTER 3

SILVIA HAD NEVER BEEN so humiliated in her life.

At least that she could remember.

Her brother, who should have her back, and one of his best friends, Grizz—the guy who'd stopped her from face-planting at the charity gala the other night—had thought it a good idea to send her to the middle of nowhere—a.k.a. Lost Creek, Texas—to a women's recovery ranch.

"Recovery from *what?*" she'd asked Axel.

They'd been at a meeting at her mom's, and four serious pairs of eyes had stared her down. Brighton, Axel, Grizz, and her mom.

Apparently, Grizz's cousin had gone to this women's recovery center to heal from the loss of her child. Right. The loss of a child was a hard thing, a traumatic event. Silvia wasn't dealing with anything even close to that. Just an overprotective brother and difficulty finding her passion in life. If everyone wasn't always comparing her to her brother, maybe she'd find it. And maybe the panic attacks would stop.

Silvia was chalking up her agreement to this whole fiasco to her guilt. Guilt for lying to her brother about dropping her classes, guilt for lying to her mom about dating yet another loser, and guilt for lying to Brighton—who'd become her closest friend—and not keeping her in the loop about how her stress levels had skyrocketed.

Thus, the panic attack at that gala.

No, it hadn't made her pass out. Dehydration and standing up too fast had done that. Oh, and maybe the racing heart and pulse from her hatred of speaking in front of people.

Which Axel had sprung on her, so it was *his* fault, right?

And it was currently his fault she was hitchhiking straight out of the small town of Lost Creek. She wasn't going to any "recovery" center. It wasn't like she was on any substances or needed an intervention. She just needed her own life—away from her brother.

So when they'd stopped to fill up gas, and Axel went in to buy who knew what, Silvia had simply climbed out of his rental car. Grabbed her suitcase. And started walking.

She was regretting her choice of footwear. But she hadn't planned on walking so far when they'd boarded the plane that morning—first class, of course. Nothing but the best for her brother.

To be fair, he was a decent guy. Just too involved in her life.

No more, she'd decided. Even if she had to find some menial job to support herself, she'd do it. She couldn't go back to that college—wouldn't. And she was pretty sure she'd fail at hair school, too. So why even set herself up for that?

Somehow, her brother succeeded at everything in life. At college, at baseball, at relationships . . . while Silvia just existed. Took up space.

Her eyes burned with tears. Now wasn't the time to feel sorry for herself. Especially when a truck had just turned around and was slowing down. Who in their right mind would pick up a sobbing hitchhiker?

She was at an all-time low, that she knew, but that didn't mean she needed to be shipped off to a recovery center with women who had serious problems they were working through. Yet, maybe she was out of her mind, too—hitchhiking. With all the news stories out there on staying safe and being smart, well, Silvia Diaz was at it again. Making another dumb decision.

Well, she was already this far . . .

She turned as the truck came to a rumbling stop. It was in need of a paint job and general maintenance altogether. In fact, she was surprised the thing was running. This was obviously one of those cowpokes who had nothing better to do with his time than drive twenty miles per hour on a back country road. Yet, the truck had come from the direction of the highway. Maybe it had gotten up to thirty-five miles per hour there.

The person inside the truck was indistinguishable for now, and Silvia headed toward the driver's side as stubbornness battled against her racing pulse, while her brain screamed: *This isn't a good idea. You're alone. A single woman. The driver could be anyone.*

Well, if the driver looked like a creep, she'd keep walking. She breathed in. Breathed out. She could do this.

Let Axel panic and miss *her*. Let him understand once and for all he didn't control her. Let him regret—

The driver popped open his door, and a young man climbed out. Well, she guessed him to be in his late twenties, at least several years older than she. And he was a total hick, uh, cowboy, if she ever saw one. From his well-worn cowboy hat tipped forward so that his eyes were a murky green in its shadow to a plaid shirt that looked like it had seen better days—*much* better days. And his jeans were scuffed, with holes at the knees that weren't a fashion statement.

But his boots took the cake. No doubt they hadn't been cleaned for a while, if ever.

She expected him to smell like a barn, or a hay field. Instead, the hot Texas breeze only sent the smell of clean soap her direction. Okay, so maybe he wasn't a complete caveman.

"How can I help you, ma'am?" he said.

That voice. The rich rumble was smooth and deep. And not exactly Texan, but he definitely had a southern drawl of some sort. It was a pleasing voice, and she could almost ignore that he'd called her "ma'am" like she was some middle-aged woman.

"I need a ride to the airport," she said. Her voice sounded squeaky, though, like she was sixteen or something. She gripped her suitcase handle tighter. "You heading there, cowboy?"

Her face flamed—well, more than it already was in this Texas heat. Why had she called him "cowboy"? She'd probably just said something offensive.

But the man standing a few feet from her didn't seem offended. Instead, he folded his arms. "Where you comin' from, ma'am?"

"First of all, I'm not a *ma'am*," she shot out. "And second of all, does it matter where I'm coming from? I need a ride. Plain and simple."

He dipped his chin. "Right." His gaze studied her.

She didn't look away. She supposed that under that worn-out hat of his, he might be considered handsome. To some women. He had a rather impressive scar along his jaw, but it sort of added to his rugged appeal. And the sandy-blond scruff along his jaw and chin made him appear as if he took little thought to his appearance. He was just one of those men who had charisma without even trying.

Or maybe she was too dang hot standing on this Texas roadside.

She sure hoped his truck had a working air conditioner.

He was still watching her, and she continued to hold his gaze.

"Hop in, then." He moved closer. "I'll put the suitcase in the bed of the truck."

She stepped back, her grip tight on the handle.

When he paused, and their eyes locked again, she saw all sorts of questions and doubts in the murky green color.

"Or you can keep it with you up front," he said, his voice low. "Might be a bit tight, though."

She exhaled, then released her grip on the suitcase. "You can put it in the back."

"Yes, ma'am," he said, then cleared his throat. "Miss."

"Miss" wasn't much better. That made it sound like she was ten years old. "You can call me Silvia, I guess."

His mouth quirked. "Will do. And my name's Westin Farr."

Of course, it was. Went along with his plaid shirt, worn jeans, and ancient cowboy boots persona.

"One more question, Silvia. How old are you?"

She wanted to tell him it was none of his business, but then some logic clicked into place. "Twenty-four."

He nodded.

"Well, Mr. Farr, I don't have all day."

"Call me Westin."

She headed around the front of the truck to the passenger door. She thought she heard him chuckle, but she didn't turn to find out.

The truck did have air conditioning inside, thank heavens, and the interior was nicer than she expected. The seat cushions were worn, but not ripped or stained. And the inside of the cab didn't smell like a barn or wet dog, or something worse. No, it smelled like . . . pine? Something woodsy.

His phone sat in the middle of the front bench, and it seemed like he had an active text strand going on by the buzzing that was taking place. The radio was on low—country music playing, of course. A *thunk* told her he'd loaded her suitcase, and a moment later, he swung up into the driver's seat.

Now, she knew he was tall, six feet at least, but in the smaller space of the cab, he seemed to take up more than his fair share.

"Buckle up, Silvia." He clipped on his seatbelt. The kind that only went horizontal.

She reached for the seatbelt, but it was either too short or stuck. She tugged harder, to no effect.

"Hang on, Silvia," Westin said. "Sometimes that one gets caught." And without asking her permission, he leaned over her and grasped the end of the seatbelt, then yanked it hard.

The thing came free from whatever clutches it had been in.

But Westin didn't stop there. Apparently, he wanted to make sure for himself that she was buckled in tight, because he did it for her.

All right, then.

She was too surprised to protest. And next thing she knew, he was pulling out onto the road. They bounced over a couple of ruts, then the pavement grew smooth.

"I can pay you, you know," she said. "If this is out of your way, that is."

He cut a glance at her, and those green eyes seemed lighter now. "It's definitely out of my way, Silvia, but there's no charge."

Why did he keep saying her name? She was trying to decide if it annoyed her. She'd never heard her name spoken in a twang, and it was kind of sweet.

"Thank you for that." Maybe she'd leave a twenty dollar bill on the seat before she got out at the airport. Did she even have cash? They'd left in such a hurry so she wasn't sure.

She dug into her shoulder bag and found her wallet. Her phone showed three missed calls. All from Axel. Whatever.

Before she could open her wallet, Westin slammed on his brakes.

"What in the world?" he muttered.

Silvia snapped her gaze up. The little red car that her brother had rented had pulled in front of Westin's truck and was blocking the way. "Just drive around him."

"You know this guy?" Westin asked as Axel climbed out of the front seat and strode toward the truck.

Her brother looked pissed, all right. His ballcap was turned backwards, and his dark eyes flashed. Yeah, her brother could be formidable, both on the baseball field and in real life. But that didn't mean he could bully her.

"He's my brother," Silvia said. "Please keep driving. Nothing good will come of this."

Westin seemed to hesitate, and for an instant, she thought he was going to gun the truck's engine and roar past her brother.

Instead, he put the truck into park and opened his door.

CHAPTER 4

THIS MAN WAS LOOKING for a fight. Westin could see that a mile away. But the guy—Silvia's brother—wasn't a mile away. He was a few yards, and in seconds, Westin might be finding himself in the middle of flying fists.

Right now, he didn't know whose fists would be flying first. Silvia was twenty-four, or at least he hoped she was telling the truth, and this guy... well, Westin had just landed himself in the center of a family feud, apparently.

"What the hell do you think you're doing?" the dark-haired man said.

But the guy wasn't talking to Westin.

He heard the snap of the truck's door locks behind him. From Silvia.

And that's when Westin recognized the irate man, as several things clicked into place. Silvia's *Sharks* baseball shirt. This dark-haired man, whose face matched none other than Axel Diaz, was one of the top shortstops in the MLB.

What was he doing in Lost Creek? With his sister?

Then Westin knew.

Kellie's women's recovery place must be their

destination—well, Broken Hearts Ranch, to be exact. Whenever there was an out-of-town woman in the area, she was usually a client at the recovery ranch.

"You've gone too far, Silv," Axel called, his voice strained, veins in his neck bulging. He detoured from Westin and headed toward the truck where his sister was barricaded.

"Hold up," Westin said, stepping between Axel and the truck. "Let's all be civil here for a moment. No reason to get the cops involved."

Axel Diaz, if this was really him and Westin wasn't in the middle of some bizarre dream, fully focused on him. "Cops? You gonna call the cops on me, man?"

Westin raised his hands. "I don't want to. Not at all. But I'm not going to allow you to badger your sister, either."

Axel's eyes widened, but he didn't move, except for the tick of his jaw. "Who are you?'

"Westin Farr."

Axel took a step closer. "I mean, who *are* you, and why is my sister in your truck?"

Westin set his hands at his waist. "She was hitchhiking. Said she needed a ride to the airport."

Axel scoffed. Then his brows pulled together. "Really?" His tone was much calmer now, and his breathing had deescalated.

Good signs for Westin. Maybe this wouldn't come to a brawl, after all. He stepped aside. "Ask her yourself."

Both men turned toward the truck. From his viewpoint, Westin could see that the truck was still locked.

"I guess she's mad at you?" Westin ventured.

"Yep."

Both men continued to stare. Silvia was sitting in the driver's seat now, her arms folded, her cold glare directed at her brother.

Westin's heart gave a little jolt. She was in *his* truck, with *his* keys, with the doors locked. There was nothing to stop her from taking off.

"Look." Westin rubbed at his jaw, then adjusted his hat, while keeping his eye on his pride and joy. That truck had been with him through thick and thin. "I don't want to get in the middle of a family dispute, but that young lady in there is under some duress. Is there something you can compromise on?"

Axel puffed out a breath. "My sister isn't much of a compromiser," he muttered.

Westin felt a laugh tickle inside his chest. "Yeah, I kind of got that impression."

Axel's mouth curved.

And Westin chuckled.

Axel extended his hand. "I'm Axel Diaz. Nice to meet you, although the circumstances are less than ideal."

Westin gripped the man's hand. "Pleasure to meet you, too, sir. Great season you're having."

Axel's brows shot up. "You follow baseball?"

Westin grinned. "Don't look so surprised. I might be a bull rider, but baseball is America's pastime."

Axel's brown eyes warmed at that. "A bull rider? Impressive."

And for some reason, that made Westin's heart happy.

"You from around here, Westin?"

"Not exactly." Westin took off his hat and swatted at a fly that was being too friendly. Then he replaced his hat. "From Oklahoma, actually. Although I went to Sam Houston Community College not far from here. Lost Creek was our home rodeo arena. There's a rodeo this weekend I'm joining in."

"You're riding bulls?"

"Yes, sir."

"Wow, if I wasn't due to be back in Seattle tonight, I'd stay and watch," Axel said. "I don't know the last time I went to a rodeo."

"Well, if your plans change, you've got a front row ticket next to the bucking chutes—"

"Really?" Silvia yelled through the open window. "You're best friends now? Leave me in the truck to rot, why don't you? While you shoot the bull! Unbelievable. You, sir, are no better than my brother."

Westin stared at her for a half-second. She was calling *him* out?

Silvia Diaz was a force to be reckoned with when she was fiery mad. Her eyes blazed, her cheeks flushed pink, and her hair . . . it had gone wild, as if she'd stuck her finger in one of those electrical sockets. But she looked tiny in his truck. All five or so feet of her was no match for the red behemoth she sat in. If she did decide to make a dead run for it, he wasn't sure if she could even see all the way over the steering wheel.

He didn't mean to—and he couldn't speak for the reaction of baseball star Axel Diaz—but Westin started to laugh, and he couldn't stop.

Axel joined in.

"This is officially the worst day of my life," Silvia continued at full volume. "Now I have *two* brutes in my life, and I'm getting nowhere sitting here."

The truck door opened, then slammed shut.

Westin winced at the treatment of his baby, but he was still trying to gain control of his laughter.

When Silvia climbed up on the tailgate in those high heels of hers, intent on getting her suitcase, Westin finally sobered.

"Now, hold up," he said, jogging over to her. "You're gonna slip in those fancy shoes of yours."

"Leave me alone," Silvia shot out just as her right foot skittered off the tailgate.

Westin was right beneath her, and he caught her about the waist as her other shoe followed suit.

"You okay, miss?"

Her petite size was deceptive. This woman was stronger than an ox.

She twisted out of his grasp before he could catch his own balance. He had to reach for the back of the truck to steady himself.

Silvia folded her arms and met his gaze, hers hot and livid.

"Please give me my suitcase back," she said in a dead-even voice. "I'll manage on my own."

Axel reached them. "Silv, come on. Let's talk this through." He flicked a glance at Westin. "In private. We don't need to involve others in our business."

But his sister didn't relax her stance. "I told you, Axe, this has to be my decision. Not yours."

Axel rubbed the back of his neck. "We already talked about this. Remember? With everyone, and you agreed—"

"I didn't agree to anything," she said. "I told you the truth. Finally. And the truth hurts, I know. Just because I'm not on the college track or dating whatever preppy dude you approve of, doesn't mean I'm a screwup. I don't belong in a place with addicts and women who are one step away from jail."

Westin's ears were ringing; he really should let these two siblings be. If there was one thing he learned from having a mom and sister, it was to never, ever take sides. His smartest move was to listen and never give advice. After an argument, his sister and mom would be bosom buddies again in another day or two, and Westin would be left completely bewildered.

But here, now, he had to say something. He knew enough about Kellie Prosper's ranch to know it wasn't a drug rehabilitation center. In fact, he'd read some of the literature. On his last visit to Lost Creek, he'd attended one of their dinner events right before the rodeo. Had met some very nice women. One was dealing with the loss of a child, the other had been in an accident that resulted in the loss of one of her hands. Every woman he'd met was dealing with grief, change, and redefining the direction of their lives.

No one had a jail sentence hanging over their heads.

"Hold up," he said, lifting a hand. "If I might say a thing or two."

Silvia turned her heated gaze on him, and if she'd had a hot poker, he wouldn't be surprised if she would have gladly stabbed it in his heart. Axel's gaze was quite different—his was desperate, as if he were a man in need of a lifeboat in a raging river.

"Are you talking about Broken Hearts Ranch, run by Kellie Prosper?" Westin said.

Silvia blinked, and Axel nodded, then said, "That's the one."

"Of course, you've heard about it," Silvia bit out. "You being a cowboy and all. Tell my brother that I won't fit in." The angry heat from her eyes had switched on a dime to a desperate, pleading look that was rightfully tugging at Westin's heart.

He had to look away from her. Stop being a softy toward this beautiful, petite woman.

"I've met several of the women at the ranch." Westin lowered his voice and focused on Silvia's deep brown eyes. "They're not addicts or one step away from a jail sentence. In fact, one recent resident is a retired veteran. They're lovely women who just need a new beginning, a second chance.

Kellie Prosper gives that to them. They come out here, in the middle of nowhere, away from their former heartaches, and well... they begin to heal."

He continued, "Kellie Prosper is one of the most kind-hearted, intelligent women I know, and her brother, Ryan, is one of my best friends. We went to college together right up the road, and we both rode for the rodeo team. Did all our training here in Lost Creek—a town that's small enough to spit across. But rodeo has been in its blood for generations, and it's as decent a town as you'll find anywhere in Texas."

Both siblings were staring at him. Axel nodded for Westin to continue. Silvia didn't look exactly pleased, but at least she wasn't yelling at her brother anymore.

Westin continued, and for some reason, he hoped Silvia would change her mind. There was so much anger in her young self, making it plain to him that she was hurting something fierce, and it went deep. "Ryan was injured a while back in a bull ride. His career is over with. You can say if anyone in Lost Creek has a broken heart, it's him. And his sister, Kellie? She's a sweetheart if there ever was one. Has her own tragic past to get over. Lost babies to miscarriages, then her husband decided he'd had enough and left her."

Silvia bit her lip, her brows tugged together as if she was trying to take in all that he was saying.

Westin swallowed, his throat suddenly papery. "If there was a place for guys, I'd go there in a heartbeat. Instead, I travel the country, just me and my truck, beating up my body riding bulls. I don't know if I'm chasing my father's ghost or running from it." He tried to smile, but it didn't happen. "Kellie has already told me in no uncertain terms, no men allowed in her therapy groups."

"I'm sorry about your dad," Axel said, clapping a hand on Westin's shoulder.

And the crazy thing was, even though Axel Diaz was a hotshot pro-baseball player, he was more sincere than most of the people Westin had met in his life. "Thanks, man."

Silvia turned and walked away, then stopped. Turned back.

Both men watched her.

"I'll go for one week, then decide from there," Silvia said, her voice so soft that Westin wasn't sure he'd heard her right.

But apparently he had, because Axel stepped toward his sister, scooped her into a big bear hug, and whooped. "Yes!"

She let a reluctant smile escape and hugged him back.

Westin might have gotten a speck of dust in his eyes that made them watery. It seemed it was all's well that ends well among the siblings.

CHAPTER 5

SILVIA HAD BEEN HOODWINKED.

That pretty talk from Mr. Cowboy-slash-bull-rider had somehow softened her heart, and now she was staring at a sparse room where the closet was no bigger than three feet across. And there was literally nothing but a bed, a rustic, worn-down night stand, a single lamp, and a braided rug on the floor. What was this, 1940?

Oh, and the bathroom was *shared*. Down the hall, and she'd already noticed the leaking faucet.

Now, Silvia didn't believe she was a spoiled woman. No, she'd had her share of challenges in life. So what if her brother was fabulously wealthy, and she'd never really lacked for material things? That didn't soothe any part of her emotional trauma or insecurities, that she knew. She had no memory of her father. She'd had a string of boyfriends who'd broken her heart more times than she could count. Darren the most recent. He hadn't even come to see her in the hospital when the paramedics had taken her there from the gala—overkill in her mind. Then there was the utter reality of being unable to make something of herself. By herself. Independent of a successful brother.

So, here she was, staring at her battered suitcase sitting on a patriotic quilt, as sounds from the kitchen filtered down the hallway. They'd told her to wash up. Two of the women had given pointed looks at her footwear. And then she was expected to join these complete strangers who were all older than her and help with dinner. Probably do the dishes, too.

Silvia sank on the bed.

Great. It was hard as a rock. Well, maybe not that hard. An hour or two on this bed would give her sore muscles. Speaking of being sore, her feet were killing her. She kicked off her scuffed and dusty high heels, then with a sigh, unzipped her suitcase. She pulled out a pair of socks and name-brand running shoes. They'd have to do. They were comfortable, and she didn't think her designer sandals would fare too well at the ranch.

All she'd seen driving up with Axel had been fields, dirt, and more dirt. The "town" part had passed by in a blip.

Axel hadn't been too happy that she'd made him stay in the car while she went to check in. She didn't want to watch a bunch of broken-hearted women ogling her superstar brother, getting their hopes up for a sugar daddy. Even if she told them he was happily married, that didn't deter some females.

Kellie was nice enough, Silvia supposed.

Her blue eyes were friendly, inquisitive.

Once Silvia verified everything was in order for her to begin her stay, she went onto the front porch and waved off Axel. He'd called goodbye and told her he loved her from the rental car window. Silvia felt a twinge of regret mixed with gratitude for her brother as he drove away.

He'd always been there for her, in good times and bad.

On one hand, she knew he wanted the best for her—always. But sometimes she needed to fall, then pick herself back up on her own.

So, was this the magic place to do it all? To stand on her own two feet? Set boundaries? Stop being co-dependent on her brother?

The whitewashed walls of the tiny room had no answers for her.

Something smelled good, and the scent grew stronger. Barbeque meat, if she were to guess.

Silvia's stomach rumbled, and even though they'd sat in first class on the flight, she'd hardly touched her meal. Who could blame her? No one had an appetite while heading to their doom.

She tied her shoelaces, then rose to her feet, her stomach propelling her into action.

Her phone beeped before she could head to the bathroom, though. Taking it out of her bag, she frowned at the incoming text. Her mom.

Love you, honey. I hope you're having fun!

Fun?

At a recovery center?

Even though that cowboy named Westin had said it wasn't for addicts, this place still wouldn't be *fun*.

Silvia gritted her teeth as she wrote back: *Thanks, Mom. Love you.*

Her mother never said a mean thing, ever. She was always bright and positive, and it honestly wore Silvia out. Her mom was an expert at keeping any negative emotions buried, always pretending things were fine. In fact, as a child, Silvia had thought her dad had ridden off on the proverbial white horse into the sunset. Until one night when Axel had told her the truth about their father.

How he used to beat their mom and Axel. How her brother finally stood up to him and called the cops. How he'd been hauled off, then released. And that's when their bank account had been cleaned out. No one had heard from him since.

For all Silvia knew, her dad could be living in a tiny town like Lost Creek. Maybe working at a rodeo or the gas station. Drinking himself into oblivion each night to forget that he had a wife and two kids.

A bell rang, and Silvia jolted from her memories that were getting very close to self-pity. An easy road for her to go down when she was alone like this. It wasn't like she was going to Instagram her story at the recovery ranch. They didn't allow pictures, anyway—Silvia had signed the nondisclosure.

"Dinner's on," someone hollered.

No peace and quiet in this place, it seemed.

At least the reward would be whatever smelled amazing. Silvia put her phone away, then stopped in the bathroom for a minute before heading into the kitchen. The table was set with plates and mugs and heavy silverware, along with napkins and salt shakers. No skimping here. Four women were busy in various stages of preparing food, although it looked like it was mostly done.

"Can you fill that pitcher with water, hon?" a woman of about fifty asked. Her short hair was spiked with gray, and her red-framed glasses made her look like a stylish librarian.

The name *Glory* popped into Silvia's mind. They'd already been introduced.

"Sure thing," Silvia said, although her voice sounded scratchy for whatever reason. She picked up the surprisingly heavy metal pitcher, then moved to the refrigerator, looking for a water dispenser.

"Oh, we just use tap water," Glory said with a chuckle. "No fancy filtered water out here."

Silvia smiled, but inside, she felt dumb. There was no ice or water outlet on the fridge at all, so she should have put two-and-two together.

"You go, girl!" someone bellowed from outside, but the sound was loud and clear in the kitchen.

Silvia turned with a start to see two women clomp into the kitchen in heavy boots. A thin woman with raven hair was grinning like she'd won the lottery, and the redheaded, curvy woman behind her had her arms raised in the air as if she was in the middle of a victory dance.

"Dirty boots at the door!" someone else hollered. *Kellie.* She flashed Silvia a grin. "Rule number one. If they're not clean, they're not coming in."

The redhead who'd done the bellowing said, "Hardly! Rule number one is no cross talking."

"That's for group," Kellie said, a laugh in her tone. "But it might be nice if you cut down on cross talk at the dinner table."

"Right," Glory said. "I'm not holding my breath."

Someone laughed.

The redhead unceremoniously pulled off her boots, then her eyes landed on Silvia. "Well, toot my horn. We got us a hatchling."

Silvia had no idea what cross talking meant, or why this redhead would call her a . . . hatchling.

"I'm Vonnie," the woman said, crossing the room and extending her hand.

Silvia put the pitcher on the table, then shook the woman's hand. It was like shaking a man's hand—a sturdy farmer's, to be exact. "I'm Silvia Diaz."

"Ah, the baseball player's sister."

Silvia's stomach felt like she'd swallowed a rock. "Uh, yep. That's me."

"Knock it off," the black-haired woman said. "No one likes to be identified by their brother. You should know that."

Vonnie looked up at the ceiling, her mouth moving, as if she were counting. When she met Silvia's gaze, she said, "Sorry about that."

Silvia had no chance to respond because Kellie clapped her hands together. "The food is half-cold, ladies. Sit down, or I'm eating your portion."

It seemed that Kellie's words weren't really threats or commands, as no one really moved that fast.

"I'm Lidia," the dark-haired woman said. "And I had a bounty hunter track my ex-husband down today, and now he's been arrested for money laundering my trust fund."

"Booyah!" Vonnie said.

Lidia laughed. "Just got word, and Vonnie was with me."

"Wow," Silvia said. She wasn't even sure she knew what money laundering was, but she definitely knew what a trust fund was. She had one herself. "Congratulations!"

"Heck yeah!" Vonnie said.

"That's amazing," Glory added, coming over to hug Lidia.

"Well done." Kellie hugged her as well.

Lidia beamed at the attention, and once they were seated, Kellie said, "I'll say grace."

The women all bowed their heads and grasped hands. As Kellie prayed, Silvia peeked at the others. Pam sat opposite, the one closest to her age, but she was still at least thirty. She hadn't said a word except for "hello" when they were first introduced. Pam's blonde hair was so pale, it was almost white.

Emma was at the other end of the table by Kellie. Emma seemed pretty good-natured. Her auburn hair was braided, and her fake eyelashes were a bit spidery. Maybe she needed new ones. She smiled a lot, reminding Silvia a little of her mom. Put on a happy face, and everything was fine.

All in all, there were six women in residence—seven if they counted Kellie.

The food was passed around the table, and Silvia took smaller helpings. She didn't know how much the other women would take. It all looked delicious, though. Diced potatoes in some sort of cream, corn on the cob, salad heavy on cucumbers and tomatoes, and of course, steaming barbeque chicken.

Her first bite should have tasted like heaven, based on the smell alone. But when she chewed, she couldn't help but make a face.

"Something wrong, hon?" Glory asked, genuine concern in her tone.

Everyone stopped in their conversations and looked at Silvia.

She brought a napkin to her mouth, embarrassed now. The meat was dry, the barbeque sauce water—no real flavor—and she couldn't seem to swallow. She gave a nod and mumbled, "Mm-hmm."

But everyone kept watching her, so Silvia forced down the swallow, although it felt like an insult to her palate. Then she reached for her glass of water and gulped some down.

"Sorry," she said, her eyes starting to water now.

Still, no one looked away. They were waiting for an explanation.

"I've just never had Texan barbeque before, I guess?" she ventured. "It's different." Bland. Tasteless.

"Oh, this isn't Texan," Glory said, a proud note in her voice. "It's my momma's recipe."

Silvia nodded and tried to smile. Maybe the potatoes were better. *Please* let them be better.

"Oh, well, then," Silvia said. "I guess I'm used to a little more spice—you know, some kick. And less, um, baking time." Now, why did she have to go and say that? *Be quiet, Silvia.*

Slowly, Glory's pleased smile faded. "You don't like my momma's chicken?"

"It's fine, really," Silvia backtracked. *I'll just need a glass of water with each bite.* She reached for the water and took another swallow, as if to soothe her subconscious. In a gallant effort, she ate another bite of chicken, since Glory was still looking at her like Silvia had just kicked the woman's puppy.

She chewed. And chewed. Swallowed. Hid a gag. Drank more water.

"Well, if we're voting on anything tonight," Glory said in a tight tone, "I vote that Silvia is in charge of dinner tomorrow right before the rodeo."

The table went silent again. No one seemed to know how to react. Had Silvia breached some serious protocol here by not loving Glory's chicken?

Kellie jumped in. "That would be fine if Silvia agrees to it. But it's Glory's week overseeing dinner, and we can't pass on our responsibilities. No matter the setbacks."

Everyone was silent again. Every pair of eyes was on Silvia again.

Her neck heated up. She didn't want to go against protocol of the recovery program or upset Glory. Cooking was probably the only thing Silvia could do well. But she'd never cooked for anyone outside of her family. Not even the guys she'd dated, because they weren't really someone she'd bring home to her mom—and never her brother.

She met Kellie's gaze. "I'm happy to cook tomorrow."

CHAPTER 6

THE FIRST FEW MOMENTS of a rising sun were the best part of the day, in Westin's opinion. Ryan had offered a bed at his place, and that's where the other guys were staying. But Westin liked things quiet—really quiet.

He turned his head as the sound of birds began to filter down from the nearby trees. The sky was violet and orange, and at any moment, the sun would spill across the far horizon. Westin didn't move, didn't hardly take a breath, as he waited. And watched.

Another bird trilled.

And there it was.

Gold bloomed at the point of the rising sun, turning the sky brilliant. More birds chattered; it seemed they were enjoying nature's finest as well.

Whatever was going on in his life, whatever disappointments, whatever aches or bruises, however much his missed his dad, the sight of the rising sun always gave Westin a new sense of hope. A fresh start for a new day.

The sound of thudding footsteps drew his attention, and he turned his head toward it. From his position where he laid beneath his pickup truck, Westin caught a glimpse of someone jogging toward the truck.

Maybe not jogging. More like running. Through a field at dawn? Why off the road?

"No, no, no," a woman's voice muttered, accompanied by fast breathing.

He scooted out from under the truck, where he'd spent many a nights on the road. It came in handy when he didn't want to stop for a hotel, or worry about getting rained on if he slept in the bed of the truck. The inside of the cab was too cramped for his long legs.

Westin spotted the jogger. Still running. The woman with long, dark hair sped past him and around to the other side of the truck. Something about her was familiar, but then his attention was redirected.

Here came Maggie at a pretty decent gallop. One of Ryan's more spirited mares. She was still young, but once she matured, she'd be an excellent barrel racer. And apparently... she was chasing the dark-haired woman.

"Whoa, hold up," Westin said, raising his hand as he strode toward the horse. Maggie slowed down as she neared the truck.

Her breath flared her nostrils, and her sides heaved.

"Where you goin', Maggie girl?" Westin said, approaching, then placing a hand on the horse's neck. Her pulse was thundering, and he stroked her neck, trying to calm her. "What's got you all worked up?"

"You know that horse?" the woman said from the other side of the truck.

Now that Westin felt free enough to look over, he recognized the woman. *Silvia Diaz.*

Similar to the last time he saw her, less than twenty-four hours ago, she was out of sorts. But this time, for a different reason.

She stood near the tailgate now, her forehead damp with perspiration, and her ponytail with flyaways. She wore a fitted tank shirt and pink running shorts. Which made her as pretty as a picture, in Westin's opinion. And if this was a bigger Texas town, he wouldn't exactly agree with her out running at dawn by herself.

"This is Maggie," Westin said. "She's one of Ryan Prosper's horses."

Silvia's brown eyes narrowed, her hands gripping the edge of the truck. "I was out jogging, and she started chasing me. Is that normal? A horse chasing a human?"

Westin hesitated, then looked at Maggie. "Were you chasing Miss Diaz?"

The horse looked completely innocent of any misdeeds.

When Westin looked back to Silvia, she'd folded her arms. "You're seriously asking the horse a question?" she asked, her voice raising in pitch. "You saw for yourself. The horse was *chasing* me. That's gotta be dangerous. What if she'd knocked me down or something?"

Westin tried to picture it in his head, but he couldn't. Maggie wasn't a wild horse, only spirited. If anything, she was probably just joining in the fun of running with someone else. "Maggie's young, and she was trying to interact with—"

"By chasing me and nearly giving me a heart attack?" she shot back.

Now, if you asked him, Silvia Diaz looked very healthy, with zero potential for a heart attack. He wasn't sure how she'd take that answer, though, and he had the sense he needed to tread carefully here.

"Have you been around horses much, Miss Diaz?"

"Silvia."

He nodded. "Silvia."

She exhaled, still a bit shaky. "Not really. I mean, I once did a horseback riding lesson, but that didn't go well."

As Westin continued to stroke Maggie's neck, she dropped her head and began to graze. Adventure over, she was now hungry.

"What happened?" Westin found himself asking—because he was truly curious. And he was finding this young woman more and more intriguing.

"Uh." She lifted a hand and smoothed back some of her flyaway hair. "Well. Axel—my brother, you know—thought it would be a fun family weekend to go to one of his friends' ranches. By the time the weekend was over, I'd twisted my ankle after trying to dismount and inhaled enough dirt to give me lung disease. Not to mention having one dopey ranch hand propose to me."

Westin barked out a laugh.

Silvia narrowed her eyes. "I was seventeen."

Westin sobered immediately. "Sorry. I hope your brother set that ranch hand straight."

Her eyes stayed narrowed. "*I* set him straight. I can speak my own mind, you know. I don't need my brother—or any man, for that matter—to rescue me."

Westin felt like he'd swallowed a burning rock. Did rocks catch on fire? "I didn't mean to imply that you couldn't speak for yourself."

She puffed out a breath and looked away for a moment.

The sky behind her was fully gold now, tinged pink and crystal blue. Westin had never seen a Texas sky so pretty.

He knew he was staring—not at the sky, at Silvia. And he should probably stop. Get on with his day. Tonight was the rodeo, and there was a lot to prepare for. First off, grab a shower at Ryan's place and change into fresh clothing. Maybe he could do a quick load of laundry there, too, before heading to the arena.

He turned to Maggie, if only to break his gaze from Silvia.

"Can I ask you a question?" she said.

This brought his gaze back to her. "Sure thing." He couldn't explain why his heart was suddenly thumping.

Her dark eyes were solely focused on him. Unlike yesterday, she didn't wear a stitch of makeup, but Silvia Diaz didn't need any.

"Were you . . . *under* your truck?"

He nodded. "Yes, ma'am."

She didn't correct his use of *ma'am*. "Did the truck break down or something?"

Westin rubbed at the back of his neck. See, he wasn't opposed to being an open book—in fact, he was more open than most guys he knew. But did he want Silvia to think he was more than the hick she surely already thought he was?

"I slept under my truck last night."

Her brows popped up. Then pulled together. "Why?"

Strangely enough, Westin had never been asked that question. His buddies would tease him about it, sure, but not ask why. Just tell him he was cheap.

Instead of giving her a quick, brush-off answer, Westin walked toward the truck and rested his forearms on the side, putting him only a few feet from Silvia. Maggie continued to graze, behaving herself.

"I like to watch the sun rise," he said. "I like the smell of dawn, and the sound of the birds. And if I sleep outside, I never miss it."

She was watching him carefully, steadily. "Under your truck in the dirt and grass?"

He didn't feel like she was mocking him, just truly curious. "Here's the thing," Westin said. "If I sleep in the bed, then I might be attacked by bandits. But if I'm under the truck, then the bandits don't see me, and I never have to worry about rain, either."

Silvia's dark eyes went through a miraculous change

then. Her cool, dark gaze warmed a few shades. Then her mouth twitched, and a second miracle happened—she smiled at him.

If cupid had stepped off a storybook page and shot an arrow into Westin's heart, he couldn't have been more stunned. Silvia Diaz smiling at him had numbed his senses and made his knees waver. Thankfully, he was leaning against the truck, so he could pretend nothing at all had happened to his insides. But he couldn't tamp down his own smile in return.

"Bandits, huh?" Silvia said.

"My daddy always told me to watch out for bandits and bad guys."

Silvia was still smiling, her voice verging on laughter. "When you were, what? Eight years old?"

"Seven."

She laughed then. A full, rich laugh.

And Westin's heart released a long, long sigh.

Who would have thought, in all the places in the entire world, he'd meet a woman in Lost Creek who could turn his head? A woman who was here at her brother's request to spend time at the women's recovery ranch?

Her gaze trailed the length of him. "I think you could take on a bandit or bad guy, maybe two or three, Westin Farr."

That she remembered his last name surprised him and made him all kinds of pleased.

"I appreciate your confidence in me."

She shook her head, her smile still filling his soul up with warmth.

"And if you're up for learning horse riding the right way, I'm happy to help you with that."

Silvia's smile faded. "I'll pass. But thank you." Her eyes darted to the placid Maggie.

"Fair enough," Westin said. The sun was nearly at the top of the horizon now, and he reached for his hat and set it atop his head. Habit whenever the sun was shining.

Silvia's gaze followed his movement, and he was pretty sure he saw a smirk flash across her face, but he wasn't about to question her about it.

"You want a ride back to Kellie's?" he asked. "I'm heading to her brother's to get in a shower, and maybe some grub if I'm lucky."

Silvia seemed to hesitate, then she eyed Maggie—who was still on her best behavior.

"I wasn't quite finished with my run," Silvia said, "but now that I'm cooled down, I think I'll take you up on that offer."

Westin headed around to the passenger side and opened the door for her.

Surprise flashed in her eyes, and Westin had to admit that he was surprised himself. Not for being a gentleman, but making things a bit more formal.

But she headed toward him, and he had to try not to stare at her too much. Her close proximity was making his pulse jump and collide as if he had a dang roller coaster inside of him.

Once she settled into the seat, he shut the door, then walked around to the driver's side.

"Behave yourself, Maggie," he said before swinging up in the truck and starting the engine. As he drove slowly along the bumpy field to the road that would take them back to the Prospers' property, Westin ventured to ask, "How did you come across Maggie in the first place?"

Silvia was looking out her window, and she glanced over at him before answering. "Oh, I always go running in the morning. Probably my one saving grace. And I thought it would be quaint to cut across this field, so I climbed over the fence. 'Maggie' seemed to be sleeping. Until she wasn't."

Westin kept his laugh to himself. It might be too soon to tease Silvia about the incident. She'd been clearly distressed. But something she'd said had caught his attention.

"What do you mean, running is your only saving grace?"

"That's a question you'll have to ask my brother, Mr. Cowboy."

CHAPTER 7

SILVIA SAW HOW THE edge of Westin's mouth curved when she called him Mr. Cowboy. Not that she was noticing. Maybe she was. She'd noticed quite a few things about him this morning.

One minute, she was sprinting toward a red truck in the middle of a field, hoping to deter the hyper horse chasing her, and the next, she was watching "Mr. Cowboy" literally take over the care of that horse. Deftly. With skill. Like he did it every day. Which he probably did.

For a man who'd slept under his truck, literally, and who hadn't showered or had his breakfast, Westin was still a fine specimen of a man, somehow.

Oh, yes, she'd noticed when she'd met him yesterday. He was all rugged charisma and could calm down a heated argument between siblings, while at the same time share a bit of his heart. When he talked about his dad, it only made her more curious about Westin. Where was he from? Had he always been a cowboy? Had he always wanted to ride bulls?

She hadn't missed that detail, nope.

It fit him, she supposed. Not that she knew any other bull

riders. She'd been to one of those indoor rodeo events once. Years ago. Axel had been hooked up with top-notch seats, and they'd gone as a family. About all Silvia could remember about it was feeling angst the entire time, since Vince had broken up with her that same day.

She'd felt wrecked and like an empty shell. Sure, there were always other fish—or guys—in the sea, but she'd been head over heels in love with Vince. Or so she'd thought. Now, she didn't even know her own mind anymore, let alone her own emotions.

Because how could she be here in teeny, tiny, Podunk Lost Creek, Texas, and be attracted to a cowboy who had grass stains on his worn jeans from sleeping in the field?

She almost laughed at her ridiculous thoughts, but thankfully choked it back. Westin Farr might as well be an astronaut trapped on the moon for all the things they had in common. Which was nothing. But he had a deep soul—and maybe that's why she was sneaking glances over at him even now. He'd gone through the loss of a dad he'd been really close to. Not that Silvia knew what it was like to have a close relationship with a father, but she was close to her mother.

Or had been.

Up until about fifteen.

Then teenage stuff got in the way—at least, that's what Silvia thought. Except, now that she was twenty-four, she still felt detached. Maybe if Axel wasn't always in their business, always providing, always "trying to help"—or dictate, whatever the case may be—Silvia and her mom would have gone through normal ups and downs and figured out things on their own.

The truck turned onto the road to the ranch. There'd been no conversation between them. It was kind of nice, Silvia decided. And for some odd reason, she felt comfortable sitting next to Westin and not having to come up with something to say. From what little she'd been around him, he wasn't a judgmental person, and that was honestly refreshing.

As Westin slowed in front of the ranch house, he said, "You doing all right at Kellie's place?"

Well. That was a loaded question.

"I'm still new," Silvia said. "But it's fine so far." She could practically feel Westin's urge to ask more questions.

Instead, he said, "Good to hear. I'm just a holler down the road if you need anything."

Silvia held back a scoff at his use of words. He was probably just being polite, anyway. "All right. Thanks for the lift." She opened her door so he wouldn't get it into his head that she'd wait for him to run around the front of the truck and open it for her.

"I'll probably see you tonight," he said.

She paused as her feet hit the ground, then looked back. "Oh, I'm not going to the rodeo."

He didn't seem fazed or offended. "I mean at the dinner here. Kellie has a tradition of feeding us rodeo boys a couple of hours before it starts."

Silvia felt the warmth from her face drain. "Tonight? Dinner?"

Westin's gaze was steady, that murky green gaze cool and smooth. "Yeah. Don't tell me you're skipping out on dinner, too?"

"Uh, no." She swallowed over the sudden hitch in her throat. "I'm assigned to cook tonight, and no one told me about . . . the extra guests."

"Well, I'll be." Westin rubbed the scruff on his jaw. "I think I'm looking forward to dinner even more now."

Silvia's face heated up again as her mind raced. How many would she be cooking for tonight? Feeding a group of women was a far cry from adding a group of cowboys into the mix. She'd found frozen meat—ribs—in the deep freeze last night and already had them thawing in the refrigerator. She planned on mixing up a few of her sauces and having more than one option of flavors. "I can't make any promises, you know. I can cook, but it's not really my saving grace."

"Like running is?"

He'd remembered.

"Yeah."

"Do you need help?" His green eyes searched her face, as if he were looking for signs of stress or an imminent meltdown. "I mean, that's quite a crowd you'll be cooking for."

"No." She didn't know every single rule of the place, but she was thinking it didn't include a hot cowboy in the kitchen. Wait . . . Had she just thought of him as *hot*? Her own face was certainly hot right now. "I'm keeping it simple. With plenty of spice, though."

Westin chuckled, his deep voice a rumble.

"Thanks again," she said in a rush, because someone had opened the front door of the ranch house, and she really didn't need an audience. She shut the truck door before Westin could reply.

Then she found herself facing Kellie, who was standing on the porch.

"Hello," Silvia said in a breezy voice as she approached Kellie.

"That's Westin, isn't it?" Kellie said, lifting a hand to wave at him.

"Mm-hmm." Silvia stepped past Kellie and walked into the house. Thankfully, she could smell coffee and something cooking. Breakfast? She seemed to be starving again.

But the footsteps behind her told Silvia that Kellie wasn't going to drop the Westin thing.

"Do you know Westin Farr?" Kellie asked.

Silvia stopped and turned before walking into the kitchen. This conversation would be better without a full audience. "We met yesterday, when, uh, my brother and I were discussing coming to the ranch. He gave us his two bits, and here I am."

Kellie's blue eyes were steady, but curious. They both knew there was more to the story, and apparently, Kellie was willing to wait.

Silvia exhaled. "I was out running just now, and he offered to drop me off back here."

Kellie blinked. "Do you run every morning?"

"Pretty much," Silvia said.

"That's great," Kellie said. "We have a built-in workout routine here. Walking after breakfast, and yoga three times a week."

Silvia nodded. "That sounds good."

Kellie smiled, although it didn't exactly reach her eyes. And Silvia thought about what Westin had told her about Kellie's losses.

"Now, grab some breakfast," Kellie said. "Eggs are ready. I was about to come holler for you, but then I saw the truck."

"Sure thing." Silvia turned away, but then Kellie grasped her arm.

Silvia looked back at the woman.

"Westin's one of the good guys," she said. "An honest, hardworking man, and I'd hate to see him toyed with."

Silvia opened her mouth, then shut it. Surely, Kellie wasn't implying . . . Silvia folded her arms. "I can assure you that I'm not planning on toying with anyone."

Kellie released Silvia and smiled. "We're in perfect agreement, then."

Silvia wanted to say something else, but her stomach

really needed attention. She opted for a nod to Kellie, then headed into the kitchen.

"Mornin', hon," Glory said the moment Silvia entered.

It took Silvia a moment to digest the fact that Glory was no longer upset with her. Water under the bridge, it seemed. "Good morning," Silvia said. "What can I help with?"

"Cleanup," Glory said at the same time as Vonnie.

Both women laughed.

"You look bright and spunky this morning," Vonnie said, her voice an octave lower than Silvia remembered. Probably due to the early morning hour.

"I went jogging," Silvia said.

Both women scowled.

"You and your young bones," Vonnie said, but there was affection in her tone.

"Now, grab your breakfast and sit here." Vonnie pulled out the chair next to her. "Tell me about your brother who plays baseball."

Silvia hid a groan. She was used to this, yes, but it got very, very old, too. Crossing to the stovetop, she scooped some scrambled eggs onto a plate, then poured a glass of orange juice. She made some toast, then put a generous helping of blackberry jam on top—with the label of BHR.

"Is this made by the ranch?" she asked Vonnie.

"Sure is," Vonnie said. "We made a large batch last week. I had berry stains for days."

By the time she sat at the table with her food, Pam and Lidia had come into the kitchen, too.

There was no avoiding this conversation, so it might as well happen around most of the women so she wouldn't have to repeat it.

"My brother is Axel Diaz, and he plays shortstop for the Seattle Sharks." Silvia reached for a blueberry muffin that was on a platter in the center of the table. "What more do you want to know?"

"How much money does he make?"

"Does he have a girlfriend?"

"How old is he?"

"Is he single?"

The questions came at her like a firehose, and Silvia raised her hand as Emma walked in, her auburn hair looking like a bird had slept in her hair last night.

"What's going on here?" Emma said. "Who are we talking about?"

"Silvia's telling us about her brother, Axel Diaz—pro baseball player," Glory announced.

"Oooh." Emma grinned. "I'm in."

Silvia exhaled and glanced over at Kellie, who was leaning against the counter, observing everyone. "My brother makes plenty of money—you can google his salary if you want. And he's married. *Happily.* I might also add that he's the reason I'm here—but I can discuss that in group therapy if you'd rather."

Everyone shut up at that.

Glory took a sip from her mug, avoiding her gaze.

"Ah, sorry," Emma murmured, her smile gone.

"We got you, sister," Vonnie said, squeezing Silvia's shoulder. "I can also break kneecaps if needed."

Pam straightened in her chair, her pale blonde hair wispy about her shoulders. "I've got a getaway car."

"My schedule is free," Lidia piped up. "Just name the time and place."

Silvia bit back a laugh. "I don't think I need to go to that extreme." She looked about the table. It felt good to have these women immediately profess they were on her side, even though they barely knew her.

Kellie moved from the counter and rested a hand on

Silvia's shoulder as she spoke to the group. "Finish up breakfast—we have group in one hour, and I expect you to walk the ranch perimeter at least twice. Get some sunshine on your beautiful faces."

Vonnie winked at Silvia, and Glory pretended to preen her spiky gray hair, and the other women laughed.

CHAPTER 8

THERE WAS DIRT, AND then there was *dirt*. The small practice arena at Ryan's ranch was a work in progress, and now the wind had kicked up, which made the dust billow about. Negating Westin's shower completely.

The Original Six had rolled in last night, and Ryan had gone all out for breakfast this morning with hotcakes, bacon, and eggs. Westin had eaten more than his fair share, then insisted on doing the cleanup. He'd also showered, not that it made a difference now. He was covered in a fine film of grit.

Right now, Reid was brushing down a horse, his dark hair peeking beneath his hat. He had the build of a wrestler, which made him the perfect bareback rider. He'd chosen the purest event to excel in—just a man and his horse.

Ford and Eric would be joining them in a couple of hours. A black truck rumbled up to the ranch, and Lars hopped out. Just in time. Lars was the oldest of the group at thirty, and he already wore a t-shirt despite the coolness of the morning. To him, Texas heat was like being forced to stay in a locked sauna for days on end.

From his truck, Lars gave Westin a nod, then turned to unload his equipment.

"Whaddya think?" Ryan said, approaching Westin where he was buckling on his leather chaps.

"The ranch looks great," Westin said. "You've put in improvements, Bulldogger." Bulldogger had been Ryan's nickname at Sam Houston.

Ryan smirked at the name, then said, "Slowly coming along. Did you see the Lost Creek arena? That's where the real work is being done."

"I did." The Lost Creek arena needed an overhaul, and when Westin had driven past, he could see that some of the rusted gates had been replaced, and there was a new coat of paint on the snack shack. Not to mention the tons of new dirt that had been hauled in. Soft as a pillow, it was. He was looking forward to riding there.

But first, some practice at this small arena of Ryan's. A few other cowboys had shown up—ones Westin had met a time or two. He bent to strap spurs onto his boots. Then he adjusted his padded vest and headed toward the bucking chute.

Ryan walked with him, and once Reid saw them heading in that direction, he left the horse he was tending to in order to join up. Lars headed over as well.

It took more than one person to get in a good bull riding practice. A couple of Ryan's ranch hands were there to help, too.

"Big Red has been waiting for you," Ryan said.

Westin laughed. "I'll bet." Ryan owned some private stock he used for practices—not for himself anymore—but he allowed other cowboys to come practice on his private property.

Westin glanced over at Reid, who'd nearly reached the bucking chute. "You wanna break him in?"

Reid scoffed. "Funny. Be my guest. Besides, I don't want to get the steers jealous that I'm switching sides."

Westin chuckled, then slowed his step as he set his sights on the waiting bull—Big Red, a black-as-night bull that was meaner than a trapped coyote. Westin knew—he'd ridden him before.

Today, though, he looked mellow. But Westin wasn't fooled. Might be early, but Big Red was still grumpy.

"We meet again," Westin muttered as he headed to the bucking chute. He mounted the beast, and Lars climbed up on the outside of the chute to help balance Westin as he steadied himself.

Sliding his right hand under the leather strap circling Big Red's girth, Westin wrapped his palm. With his other hand, he grasped the double rope and anchored it between his last two fingers.

The wind had died down, which settled the dirt.

"Ready?" Ryan asked, holding the rope attached to the gate.

Westin nodded, and Ryan tugged open the gate.

Reid waited on the other side to distract the bull once Westin finished.

Big Red was more than ready, and he flew out of the chute, rearing and twisting.

Westin was prepared for the power of the beast, though. This was just a warmup, but he took every half-second seriously. He focused on staying upright, while maintaining his balance by leaning back as far as possible. Big Red began to rotate in a circle, and still Westin held on, although his hat flew off.

"Eight!" Ryan called out.

Westin released his grip and allowed himself to separate from Big Red. The second his body hit the dirt, he scrambled to his feet and took off toward the fence.

Reid called to the bull, redirecting his ornery fury to someone other than the cowboy who'd just ridden him.

Between Ryan and Reid, Big Red made it back into the bucking chute, sides heaving, personally offended.

Westin continued over the fence and walked slowly to the bucking chute, rotating his neck. It had been a good ride, nothing that had injured him. By tomorrow morning, he'd be plenty sore. But as long as he didn't get injured tonight, he'd be good enough to drive to the next rodeo the following weekend.

Ryan was already trying to talk him into staying in Lost Creek for a few days. But Westin hadn't committed to anything. Maybe if his ex-girlfriend Amy stayed away from his neighborhood and his mom, he'd feel more settled.

"Who do we have here?" Westin asked as he approached the second bull that Lars let into the bucking chute. He was light brown, and he looked like he had fifty pounds on Big Red.

"This here is Bruiser," Ryan said.

"Because..." Westin began.

"I think you're gonna figure that out real quick," Lars said with a laugh.

"Ha. Ha." Westin deadpanned. He climbed into the bucking chute, and Lars steadied him.

"Now, show us what you got, West," Lars said. "But be quick about it. We don't have all day, and it's already hotter than a forest fire."

Westin smirked as he wrapped the rope around his hand, getting a solid grip. "It's just beginning, Lars, and it's only May. Plenty of more heat to come, Montana Boy."

Lars sighed. "I know. I just wish I had me a lady to bring me a cold drink."

Westin anchored his knees against Bruiser's side. "If that's what you think of ladies, it's no wonder you're still single at thirty."

"Speak for yourself," Lars said. "You're only a couple years behind me, and I don't see you mentioning any lady friends."

"That's because I've got some career goals."

"Stop your chattering, boys," Ryan called out.

Once Westin gave the signal, Ryan released the gate.

Bruiser practically sailed out of the bucking chute, and Westin wondered if the bull's hooves even hit the ground. Westin found himself using every bit of strength just to stay on the bull. Ryan was only to six seconds when Westin was thrown. He landed hard on his left shoulder, and he rolled immediately away from the thundering hooves. Reid moved between him and the bull in an instant, and Westin scrambled to his feet.

He hobbled to the fence, his ankle aching, but he didn't have time to do an assessment. Getting over the fence was much preferable to having a horn in his back from Bruiser.

"You okay?" Ryan called after him.

Westin hopped down on the other side of the fence and hid a wince. "Fine!" he called back. He took off his glove and swatted the dirt off his pants. His ankle ached, but it would be fine. His left shoulder was what had taken the brunt of the fall. He rubbed it, not liking how it felt. He should probably ice it for a bit before tonight's performance.

As of now, though, he was done with practice. Another spill like that, and he wouldn't be riding tonight.

The two bulls were back in their pen, along with a couple of others. The other cowboys who were bull riding could have their turn now.

"What do you need help with?" Westin asked, trying not to limp as he approached the waiting guys with their concerned gazes.

"You took a hard fall," Lars said. "Wanna get checked out at the medical clinic?"

"Nah," Westin said. "Just a good thump. Nothing broken or torn." He should know. He'd been through it all, as the scar on his jaw attested.

Lars didn't look fully convinced, but Reid had already nodded and headed off to work on his horses again.

"There's ice at my place," Ryan said, knowing exactly what Westin would be doing for the next hour. "Don't worry about us here. There's plenty to do, but plenty of hands to do it all. We'll see you at dinner."

"I'll come back in a couple of hours," Westin started to say, but Ryan cut him off.

"Dinner. And not a second earlier."

Westin grabbed his hat from where someone had set it on the post, then he slapped it against his thigh and put it back on. "Sure thing. But you got my cell if something changes."

Ryan just folded his arms, as if he were guarding the arena itself.

Westin headed to his truck and drove back to Ryan's place. No one was around the ranch. Ford and Eric must have left already. Once Westin finished his shower, he dug into the deep freeze and found a bag of ice—likely from a gas station. He propped it on his shoulder as he sat on one of the benches on the wide porch. Looking out over the ranch, Westin noticed Ryan had been putting a lot of time into his place.

Since Ryan's career-ending injury, he'd taken on a lot of different jobs. Like maintaining his own ranch and fixing up his sister's place—which had been their parents'. And the effort was now visible.

Pride swept through Westin at the thought of his friend who'd been through so much, yet had kept his nose to the grindstone and just got stuff done.

Injuries could happen to any of them, at any moment. Heck, Westin had had plenty of his own, but the recovery had only been weeks. Not months or years, or never.

Even at twenty-eight, he still had some years left of rodeo. Older guys than him continued to compete professionally. Westin just wanted to beat his dad's record, and then he'd reassess. The ranch in Oklahoma had been calling to him lately. As long as his mom and sister were doing good, he'd stay on the circuit until he reached his goal.

Even if the minor bumps and bruises seemed to last longer and longer as of late.

Westin called his sister to get an update. "Hey, Cheryl, how's it going?"

"Hi, West. You competing tonight?"

"Yep."

She gave a soft laugh. "Good luck, brother. Get a perfect score, all right? Then you can come home sooner."

"Is something going on?"

"No, you doofus," she said. "We just miss you. Mom's staying here for a couple of nights."

"Oh, good," he said, relief settling on his shoulders and taking a weight off. "I was hoping she would. I don't trust Amy."

"I'm not worried about your ex-girlfriend," Cheryl said. "What's she going to do? Crank up her music outside the house and turn her puppy dog eyes toward your bedroom window?"

"Hey—"

Cheryl snickered. "I'll tell Mom you called. She's into a new TV series. Lots of drama."

This made Westin laugh and feel about ten times lighter.

"Well, I'm sure I'll be hearing all about it soon enough."

When he hung up with his sister, his gaze shifted once again in the direction of Kellie's place.

He had no idea how many women were in residence there right now, or what they were dealing with on a personal basis. But his thoughts did center on one woman in particular. It was early yet, but he wasn't going to sit around all afternoon icing his bum shoulder. He needed to be of use to someone.

If Ryan didn't want him at the arena, then it looked like Westin would be working in the kitchen making dinner with a certain spirited woman who he couldn't quite figure out, but was enjoying trying.

CHAPTER 9

"I'M ON KITCHEN DUTY with you, I guess," Glory said, walking into the already stifling room.

Silvia looked up from where she stood at the kitchen counter, shucking corn. She'd be grateful for the help, but *Glory*? The woman who'd already clashed with her?

Although in group therapy earlier in the day, Silvia's opinion about every woman had done a one-eighty-degree turn. First impressions could be so, so wrong. She learned that in the first thirty minutes of the group session. And she'd learned a lot about herself. Yes, her brother had faults and flaws, but he was doing the best he could.

It was Silvia who wasn't.

That had been a bit hard to accept. She needed to work through her resentments, and apparently, she had a lot of them. After group, she'd spent an hour journaling—spilling words all over the page with resentments that went way back and deeper than she could have imagined. And she still wasn't finished.

Strangely, she felt lighter this afternoon, as if just sharing her burdens with the other women had already helped. She wasn't sure what to make of that, but right now, she had to focus on feeding the masses.

"Hello?"

Silvia blinked and looked at Glory.

"Wool-gathering, were you?"

Silvia was still coming out of her hazy thoughts. "I guess, sorry."

"It's okay, hon," Glory said. "I remember my first group when I arrived a couple of weeks ago. I think I cried the rest of the day."

Silvia stared at Glory—the woman was a tough nut, and she'd also imparted a lot of wisdom that had made sense.

"Don't look so shocked," Glory said, a wry smile on her face. "One of the things Kellie is having me work on is expressing emotions. And not jumping to anger as my go-to emotion."

Silvia nodded. "I think I overexpress my emotions, but my mom is endlessly cheerful."

"That sounds exhausting," Glory said.

Someone *understood.* "Yeah, it is." And dang it, her eyes filled with tears.

"Oh, hon." Glory stepped forward and hugged Silvia.

It was nice, and it only made her cry more.

When Glory released her, she said, "Now, show me some of your cooking magic. I'm here to learn."

"I don't know about magic," Silvia said, wiping at her eyes. "Like I said, sometimes I should keep my mouth shut."

Glory set her hands on her hips. "Never."

Silvia took a deep, stuttering breath. "All right. Well, how about you start on the seasoning for the corn on the cob?"

Glory pulled a face. "The *what?*"

Silvia laughed. "You'll love it. We need celery salt, onion salt, black pepper, oregano, and bacon bits."

Glory set to work, muttering to herself as to why they couldn't just use Season-All like regular folk.

Silvia smiled at she assembled ingredients for homemade barbeque sauce and let all the flavors marinate together. Then she began chopping veggies for fresh salsa while Glory was instructed to fry up corn tortillas. The chicken would need to be started in about an hour—not too early, since Silvia wanted it perfect.

She grabbed a white onion and was beginning to chop when someone knocked at the back kitchen door.

Strange to have someone knock; the women came and went as they wished. Although Silvia suspected no one would come into the kitchen unless they wanted to be roped into helping.

"Can you get that?" Glory said. "I'm up to my elbows in frying grease here. Why we need homemade tortilla chips is beyond me. There's a giant bag in the pantry—"

Silvia brushed off her hands and opened the back door as Glory continued to prattle. It wasn't any of the women, or Kellie, or even one of the ranch hands that she'd seen about the property.

No.

It was a cowboy. A bull rider, to be exact.

Westin was taller than she remembered, or maybe it was because she was barefoot. He was still wearing that old cowboy hat, and he had on a fitted t-shirt, jeans, and yep, those boots.

"Hi, um, can I help you?" Why did she feel flustered? He was probably looking for Kellie.

"How are you?" he asked, his voice a rumble, his eyes on her.

"Good. How are you?"

His mouth curved, and she almost smiled, too, at their stilted formality.

"Do you need Kellie?" How were his eyes so impossibly dark green? And it was obvious he'd showered, but not shaved.

"No. I'm here to help."

Silvia wasn't sure she understood what he was referring to. "Help?"

"With dinner." Westin looked past her into the kitchen.

"Come on in, hon," Glory said in a cheerful voice. "We can use all the help we can get. Silvia here is demanding homemade this and homemade that."

"We're fine," Silvia said. "We don't need—"

Westin walked right past her. Apparently listening to Glory. Silvia caught the scent of clean soap.

"Homemade tortillas? Wow."

Silvia wavered between rolling her eyes or allowing a little pride to work its way in. She joined them in the kitchen, sure some rule was being broken. If Kellie complained, then Silvia could say that Glory had invited him.

Might as well put the cowboy to work now that he was here. "Wanna cut the onions or make guac?" Silvia asked.

Westin took off his hat and scrubbed a hand through his short hair. Then he hung up his hat on a peg by the door that Silvia hadn't even noticed.

"Well, seeing as I'm allergic to onions, I guess I'll make the guac."

"You're allergic?" Glory asked.

"Yes, ma'am."

"Well, I'll be . . . Does your throat swell up, or you break out in hives all over?" Glory asked.

Westin chuckled. "Not exactly. I just cry like a baby."

Glory laughed, and Silvia smirked.

At least he had a creative way to get out of chopping onions.

"The avocados are there. You can peel and mash them. The limes are on the counter. You'll want about three."

Westin picked up an avocado and started to dig his thumbnail into the tough skin.

"Not like that," Silvia said. "Use a paring knife."

Westin looked up from his futile peeling. "A *what* knife?"

"Here." Silvia snatched the small paring knife from the knife block and handed it over, handle first.

Westin made a cut in the avocado, then began to peel. Once he had several peeled, he seemed to be stumped again.

Silvia scooped the chopped onions into a bowl, then started on chopping cilantro.

"Cut them in half and pop out the core pit," she said. "Once you have the avocado mashed, squeeze lime juice in to keep it from browning and to pull out the flavor. I'm almost done with the veggies."

Westin looked at the cutting board. "Lettuce?"

She couldn't tell if he was kidding. "Cilantro."

His brow furrowed, and she still wasn't sure if he was this clueless. She returned to her chopping as he mashed the avocado.

"Okay, I think that's plenty," Glory said. "Don't you think?"

Silvia looked over to see the impressive pile of fried tortillas that Glory had finished. "That looks good, thank you."

"You're welcome," Glory said. "I'm heading off to get cleaned up. Need to finish my journaling, too. I'm sure Westin here can fill in for me?"

"Sure thing," Westin said at the same time that Silvia said, "Wait, you're leaving?"

Glory only smiled, took off her apron, then hung it over a chair and walked out.

Silvia stared after her. She didn't know how she felt being alone with Westin. His presence seemed to take up every space in the kitchen, and it was hard to push him out of her thoughts when he was in the same room.

"Wow, this is good," Westin said from behind her. "What's in it?"

She spun to see him taste-testing her marinating barbeque sauce.

"Don't touch that," she said, and moved toward him.

He just looked at her, a half-smile on his face, not making any move to put down the spoon he held in his hand.

"Give that to me." Silvia reached for the spoon, but he held it out of her reach, his smile changing to a grin.

She lunged for the spoon, and he easily dodged her. But her toe caught on a chair, and the sudden, hot pain caused her to stumble.

"Whoa," Westin said, grabbing her around the waist and keeping her from falling or bumping into something else. "Are you okay?"

His mouth was so close to her ear that her hair tickled her cheek with his breathing. And . . . her back was pressed against his chest, while his arms still encircled her waist. Warm and strong.

She had no idea what happened to the errant spoon.

"I'm fine," she said, but sounded out of breath. She chalked it up to her throbbing toe.

"Is your toe broken?"

"I don't think so." She could feel the beating of his heart, as fast as hers. It was only because he'd acted so fast in preventing her fall.

"Let's have a look," he said, releasing his hold. "I know all about broken bones."

As he stepped away from her, she hoped the heat of her

face would calm down before she faced him. She didn't really want Westin touching her bare feet. It seemed so . . . personal.

But he'd already pulled out a chair. "Here, sit, let me see."

So she sat, and he knelt in front of her. His touch was gentle, and his hands were warm. She was grateful she'd had a pedicure last week, so her feet were at least decent.

"Ow!" she said, when he moved her big toe.

"Sorry," he said, his gaze connecting with hers. "It's not broken, just tweaked."

"Tweaked? Is that official medical terminology?"

Westin smiled. "It is."

Why was she smiling back? He'd almost caused her to break her toe, and now she'd be hobbling around the kitchen.

"Just like when I tweaked my shoulder today," he said, his hands still holding her foot. "Needed some ice, but it will be fine tonight."

"I don't want ice."

"Does it hurt?"

"Yeah, but not as much anymore."

Their gazes held, and Silvia wanted to think that the diminished pain had nothing to do with his warm hands.

She drew her foot out of his grasp and stood up. "All right. Where did that spoon go? Don't think I've forgotten that you broke my number one rule."

"Rule, huh?" he said, bending to grab the fallen spoon from the floor. When he straightened, they were only a foot apart.

And she could still smell his clean soap scent, mixed with lime now.

"Yes, when I'm cooking, no one taste-tests," she said. "Only me."

Westin's brows popped up. "I think it's time for a new rule."

She tilted her head, keeping eye contact. "Really?"

He grasped her hand. "Yeah."

Her heart thumped, once, then twice. "I don't think so."

"I think so," he said, still holding her hand. Was he trying to bribe her with hand-holding and warm shivers up her arm? "I think that, as your assistant tonight, I should be able to taste-test, too. After all, I'm your only help, and it's a fair trade."

She looked down at their linked hands. His was larger, rougher, stronger, but somehow warm and comforting, too. Solid. She sighed. "Okay."

"Okay?"

She nodded, meeting his gaze. "You can be a taste-tester, too, but only today."

Westin grinned, squeezed her hand, then released it. "Now, where's the spoon drawer? I need a clean one."

CHAPTER 10

WESTIN HAD NEVER SEEN so many spices and chopped things going into guacamole in his life. But to be fair, he'd never made it, either. Silvia wasn't even looking at a recipe book as she ordered him around. Chop this. Dice that. Stir. Shake.

At one point, he wondered if he'd hit his head when falling off Bruiser today, because he had no idea what she meant by "whisk".

"And how am I supposed to *whisk* this mayonnaise?"

"Get the whisk," Silvia said, not even looking at him while she deboned chicken pieces.

Maybe he should do that instead. Although it looked pretty slippery, and Silvia was making quick work of it.

Still, Westin was stumped about the whisk.

He'd poured the instructed amount of milk into a bowl, as well as the mayonnaise. Then he'd added some dried spice mix into the batch. Now, whisking? He knew it needed to be stirred, so what was wrong with a spoon? He knew right where the utensil drawer was.

He opened the drawer and pulled out a spoon, then

changed his mind and grabbed a fork. The mayonnaise was kind of lumpy.

"Here you go," Silvia said, closer to him than he'd expected. She'd risen from her chair and was standing right next to him now, holding a silver thing that looked like a tangle of wires on a post.

He couldn't hide the surprise in his eyes, apparently, because she said, "Here, let me show you."

She had that exasperated note in her tone, but he wasn't fooled. When she was mad, everyone knew it. This wasn't mad . . . This was kind of endearing. He moved to the table, where she was rotating up a mini-hurricane in the bowl of homemade dressing.

"Nice invention."

Silvia smiled without looking at him, but he knew she was *aware* of him. She had to be. He hadn't missed her blushing—more than once this afternoon. Heck, he'd almost blushed. But he was glad her toe felt better, and he was also glad that she'd accepted his help.

After Glory had left, he'd been unsure if Silvia was going to kick him out, or let him stay.

She'd let him stay, and he felt as triumphant as a rooster at dawn.

In just moments, the dressing thickened right before his eyes. "Looking good," he said. "Do you want me to try it now?"

"Almost finished," she said. "It's kind of fun to whip this up."

Westin wasn't entirely convinced of that, but he didn't mind watching her do the whipping up. He stuck a finger in the bowl, then tasted the dressing.

Silvia snapped her narrowed eyes to his, and he only smiled. "It's good. Had to be sure. You know, in case it needed more of something."

"It already has everything," Silvia said in a pointed tone.

She had no makeup on, yet her lips were a dark pink, and her cheeks had a pretty flush to them. Not to mention her dark lashes framing her dark eyes. Beautiful. Westin sort of wished they were dating, because if they were, he'd kiss her right now.

"Here." She picked up a slice of green pepper she'd had him chop for the salad. "Try this." She dipped the pepper into the dressing, then held it up to him.

"That's a pepper."

"I know."

"I don't eat peppers this way."

But she moved it closer to his mouth, and before he knew it, he'd taken a bite. He chewed. Swallowed. "Not bad." And it wasn't. He'd prefer it in a salad, but the homemade dressing would probably make a turnip taste good.

"Where are you from, Mr. Cowboy?"

"Oklahoma."

"And they don't have peppers there?"

"They sure do, but not like this." Somehow, he couldn't look away from her, and she was studying him as well.

She puffed out a breath. "What do you like to cook for yourself?"

"What makes you think I only cook for myself?" he said, unable to stop smiling at her. "Maybe I cook every night for a whole crew, or maybe just for my girlfriend."

Silvia didn't even hesitate before saying, "You don't have a girlfriend, Mr. Cowboy."

This surprised him. "How do you know?"

"Because you have moon eyes," she said, patting him on the chest, then she handed him the bowl of dressing. "This goes into the fridge."

She sat at the table and began to arrange the deboned chicken on trays.

He stared after her. "What did you say?"

She glanced up at him, her eyes filled with amusement. "You keep looking at me like you've just seen an oasis in the middle of a desert."

Westin chuckled. "Is that right?"

She didn't answer, but returned to the chicken.

He set the dressing in the fridge, then pulled out a chair and sat right next to her. In a quiet voice, he said, "Maybe you're right. But I don't think you can completely read my mind."

She paused in her work. "I've dated a lot of men. I know the look."

A lot of men? How many? Probably plenty, he assumed. But the fact didn't deter or bother him. "So you think I want to date you?"

Silvia smirked. "Dating might be a bit more extensive than what's going through your mind."

Westin slapped a hand to his heart. "You are out for the kill, aren't you? I'm a gentleman, you know."

Her brows lifted. "I'm sure you are. But I'm at a women's recovery home." She rose from the chair and lifted the tray of chicken, then carried it to the counter. "And so I think you should focus on heating up the grills outside for this chicken."

Westin picked up the second tray and followed her, then set it next to the first tray.

She moved in front of him and turned on the kitchen tap.

He stepped back, giving her a few more inches of room, but not much. When she finished washing her hands, he handed her a small towel.

Before she could step away from him, he said, "I don't know what you being in a recovery home has to do with anything."

Silvia's dark eyes held his as she tapped her head. "I'm obviously messed up here. And that's pretty significant."

Westin grasped her hand, moving it away from her head. "You're not messed up. Don't say that, or even think it."

She released a breath. "You know what I mean. And you . . . well, you're going to be riding off into the sunset once the rodeo is over."

He still held her hand, and she wasn't pulling away. "More like the sunrise," he said. "I'm leaving in the morning."

The look of surprise mixed with disappointment on her face should have been gratifying, but it only twisted his heart. He wasn't sure if it was a good twist or a bad twist.

"Oh." She drew her hand away and headed toward the back kitchen door. Outside the door sat a couple of grills. "I'll get the grills heating up if you can bring the chicken outside."

"Silvia."

She opened the door and stepped out.

He followed with the two trays of chicken and set them on a small table by one of the grills.

Two ranch dogs, with gray colored fur and black spots, were lounging in a spot of shade just beyond the patio. They immediately rose and trotted over. "Don't even think it, Casper. Frankie." Westin kept his voice firm. "Now you go back to where you came from."

The dogs paused, their eyes downcast, but both returned to their shady spot.

Westin folded his arms as he watched Silvia spark the propane and get both grills warming up. When she turned to face him, she moved a bit of hair out of her face. "Thanks for your help, but I can take it from here."

"I'm going back home to check on my mom," he said. "My ex-girlfriend called me yesterday and acted like we weren't broken up. I don't think she'd actually be a danger to my mom, but Amy has done some off-beat things in the past, so I'm going to make sure she's not hanging around the neighborhood."

"How long has it been since the breakup?"

That she was asking such a question intrigued him. And almost made him smile. "A while," he said. He didn't want to talk about Amy right now. He took a step closer. The Texas wind had stirred Silvia's hair again, shifting strands of her ponytail against her neck.

"I have a rodeo next weekend only a couple of hours from Lost Creek. If you're still here, then I was thinking of stopping by. Saying hi." He could see the questions in her eyes, and he was happy to answer any of them. At least the ones that he could. He wasn't entirely sure he knew his own mind. He was following his gut here.

"It's a free country, Mr. Cowboy."

"Sure is."

"I might not be here next weekend."

He shrugged. "I'll take that risk."

"Silvia?" someone called from inside the kitchen.

"Out here," she called back, quickly stepping away from him and turning toward the grills. She opened the first lid and had started putting on the chicken by the time Kellie Prosper stepped outside.

"There you are." Kellie's light blue eyes shifted to him. "Oh, hi, Westin. What brings you here?"

"Helping out with dinner preparations," he said, rocking back on the heels of his boots. "Since you're feeding us guys, too, I thought I'd pitch in."

Kellie only frowned. "Why aren't you at the arena practicing with the others?"

"Tweaked my shoulder," he said. "I'll be fine for tonight's ride, though."

Kellie's gaze cut from him to Silvia, then back to him. Doubt was clear in those baby blues, but she only nodded. "Well, thanks for your help. I'll take it from here, though."

"Yes, ma'am," Westin said. "Just need to grab my hat.'"

Kellie smiled. "I'll bring it out."

When Kellie disappeared into the house, Westin looked over at Silvia. Her cheeks were flushed, and he guessed it wasn't from the heat of the grill. "Did I get you in trouble?"

"Just go."

He couldn't read her tone, but he'd come this far, so he might as well take the next step. "I got you something."

She looked at him then.

He withdrew a folded rodeo ticket from his back pocket and handed it over to her. "In case you change your mind."

She didn't move, didn't reach for the ticket, so he set it on the table next to the trays of chicken. She could take it, or leave it.

"Here you are," Kellie said, stepping out, hat in hand.

"Thank you, ma'am," he said.

"Don't *ma'am* me, West."

He smiled and bent to kiss her cheek before replacing his hat. "Good day, ladies. I'll be back later for the best part."

He strode off, sure Kellie was staring after him because she was no dummy. She saw straight through him. Which apparently, Silvia had as well. It turned out he was a man who wore his heart on his sleeve. And that heart was definitely interested in Silvia Diaz.

So what if she was in recovery for whatever she had to work through? He was by no means perfect in any way. And he didn't expect anyone else to be. Except for achieving his goals as a bull rider, he was laidback overall.

His phone buzzed as he walked around the house to the front driveway, where his truck was parked. He pulled his phone out of his pocket as he reached his truck. He'd ignored his phone the entire time he was with Silvia.

An unknown caller lit up the screen. Normally, he wouldn't answer, but what if it was someone from the arena, or one of his upcoming venues?

"Westin Farr," he answered, settling into his truck and turning on the engine to get the AC started.

"Westin," the male voice said. "Glad I caught you. This is Axel Diaz. We met yesterday when I was with my sister—"

"I remember," Westin said. How was it that a pro-baseball star was calling his cell phone? "How can I help you, sir?"

"Are you still in Lost Creek?"

"Sure am," Westin said. "Rodeo is tonight."

"Oh, great, good luck with your event."

"Thank you." He waited for Axel to get to the point.

"I wondered if you could do me a favor, man," Axel said. "And I'll return it any way I can. Tickets to a game, or—"

"I'm happy to help," Westin cut in. "No return favor needed."

Axel paused. "You might change your mind when I tell you what it is."

"What's up?"

"It's my sister."

Westin wasn't surprised.

"She's, uh, she can be unpredictable," Axel said. "She was supposed to call me this morning—after her first night, you know. Check in. Tell me how she's doing. But she hasn't. So of course, I checked in with Ms. Prosper. She only said that all my communication should be with my sister because of some HIPPA law."

Westin's mind caught up. "So you want me to report on her—despite HIPPA?"

Axel didn't laugh. "Exactly."

Westin exhaled. "I don't know—"

"Not like a real report, just let me know that she's okay," Axel said. "That she's not hitchhiking her way out of there."

Both men chuckled, even though it wasn't all that funny.

"Do you have a sister?" Axel asked.

"I do."

"Then you understand how much I'm worried."

There'd be no harm in telling Axel that Silvia was fine—cooking up a storm, sassy as ever. "All right," he said. "I don't want to get anyone in trouble, though."

"You won't," Axel said. "Help a brother out?"

"Sure," Westin said. "I can tell you that she seems to be fine. She's in charge of dinner at the ranch tonight, and in fact, I was just in the kitchen helping her out with some of the cooking."

"Oh, wow." Axel's voice was filled with relief. "You don't know how good it is to hear that. What was her mood? Was she happy?"

Maybe Westin had agreed too fast. "She was . . . happy, I guess. Bossy, more like it. She's very, uh, particular with food preparation."

Axel chuckled. "Oh, perfect. I can't tell you how much I appreciate hearing this. I'll tell my mom, too. We're sitting in Seattle wondering if we made a huge mistake. Thanks, bro. I owe you. And feel free to text me with any updates. Anytime, day or night."

The guy hung up before Westin could tell him that one update had been plenty. He didn't want to be in the middle of the sibling relationship, and besides, if she didn't want to talk to her brother, there must be a reason for it.

He pulled away from the ranch house and headed toward Ryan's place. The rest of guys should be arriving soon, and in another hour, they'd all head back to Kellie's. But right now, he needed the drive to clear his head.

Silvia had seen right through him. At least that was out of the way. But what did she think about *him*? Despite them living worlds apart, would she ever be interested in a guy like him? One who was probably messed up in the head, too?

He smiled as he thought of how she'd whisked that dressing, then made him taste the green pepper. He wondered if she'd come to the rodeo tonight. It had been a long time since he'd anticipated seeing a woman show up at a rodeo. Maybe they could do some stargazing after. Watch the sun rise the next morning.

As he neared Ryan's place, Westin wondered if he should tell Silvia about her brother's phone call. Maybe he could ask her more about Axel, and then gauge it from there.

For now, he'd let her make that next move. If she showed up at the rodeo, then he'd know... And he'd ask her to spend more time with him. Somehow.

CHAPTER 11

DINNER HAD BEEN EXCELLENT, if Silvia could say so herself.

The women, and all the cowboys—six of them—had been more than complimentary. Interestingly enough, Westin had been quiet among the larger group. She'd felt his gaze on her more than once, but he only thanked her for the meal. Even when Kellie commented that he'd had a hand in preparing it, he'd just nodded.

Interesting.

Westin had been more than talkative when it was just the two of them.

Maybe he'd cooled toward her? They'd definitely flirted, and she'd even called him out—and he hadn't denied a thing.

So, what had been going through his head at dinner?

Not that Silvia should be dwelling on this.

The women were all in their rooms, getting ready for the rodeo that was going to start in an hour. One would have thought they were a bunch of giggly teenagers who were discussing high school by their conversation before everyone separated to get ready.

As for Silvia, she still wasn't going.

She hadn't even turned on her bedroom light, but instead, lay on the bed as the twilight deepened outside, and the stars popped to life, one by one. Her window gave her a great view of the western horizon.

The ticket Westin had given her was in her jeans pocket. She'd slipped it in there so Kellie wouldn't ask any questions.

A knock sounded at the door. "You still staying here, hon?" Glory called out.

"Yeah," Silvia answered.

The door cracked open, and Glory's head appeared. She was gussied up in a cowboy hat and pink boots. Silvia smiled at the sight.

"I got extra boots for you if that's holding you back," Glory said. "What size are you?"

Silvia sat up on her bed and leaned against the wall. "That's not why I'm not going."

Glory stepped into the room. "Then why not?"

"I'm just not interested in rodeo." Silvia shrugged. "I went to one once, and it wasn't that great."

"Where?"

Silvia frowned. "Does the location make a difference?"

"Sure does," Glory said. "Don't tell me you went to one of those indoor places that are purely for entertainment."

At Silvia's nod, Glory continued, "You need to see the real thing. The raw competition. The skill and talent that it takes to perform to the limit of human capacity."

Silvia blinked.

"It's better than sitting here, alone in your room, in the dark."

Maybe Glory had a point, but then she thought of Westin giving her the ticket. Quite smugly, in fact. If she went, he'd think *she* liked *him*. But then again, he was leaving in the morning, and when her week at the ranch was up, she'd be leaving, too.

"Okay, I'll come."

Glory grinned. "That's better news than a fly finding untouched honey. Come with me, I have just the thing for you to wear."

"I didn't know you had to wear something specific to a rodeo."

"You have no idea." Glory reached out and tugged Silvia's hand until she stood from the bed.

"Nothing sparkly or with sequins."

Glory only chuckled.

As they stepped into the hallway, Glory called out, "Silvia's coming, everyone! Give us a few minutes."

Well, so much for keeping things on the down-low.

"Great!" Pam said, sticking her head out of her bedroom door down the hall. She wore dark lipstick—a marked contrast to her ghost-pale skin.

Glory continued to hold onto Silvia's arm as if she was worried that she'd change her mind and flee the ranch at any moment.

Once in Glory's room, the woman began to sort through her clothes in her closet. This bedroom was nearly twice the size of Silvia's, and there was a lot more furniture in it. "How does one sign up for this bedroom?"

"First come, first serve," Glory said, flashing a smile. "When I leave, you can have it."

For some reason, that comment made Silvia feel a little panicky. She didn't want Glory to leave.

Glory paused in her search. "Don't worry, I'm here for a while yet. Gotta figure out the *new* me first."

Glory had gone through a divorce from an alcoholic husband the year before. During their marriage, she'd spent years blaming and resenting him for every wrong in her life. This morning in group therapy, she'd said she never realized that she was half of the problem and had kept their marriage chaotic because of her intense co-dependence.

"Ah, this one will work." Glory held up a dark red gingham shirt. "Look, it has cute ties at the bottom, and the color will make those dark eyes of yours stand out. Westin Farr won't be able to take his eyes off you."

Silvia felt herself flush. "It's not like that between us."

"And a fish can breathe out of water." Glory tossed the shirt to Silvia. "Try it on. And these boots." She stooped and picked up a pair of black cowboy boots that looked about a hundred times nicer than the ones Westin wore.

"This is going overboard," Silvia said. "What's wrong with what I'm wearing?"

Glory scrutinized her like she was a fashion designer in Milan. "The jeans are cute. But the baggy t-shirt has to go. Oh, and take this." She handed over a cowboy hat. Also black.

Now, Silvia's arms were full.

"And hurry," Glory said. "We've got five minutes to be in the truck, and Kellie doesn't like to wait."

Silvia got ready plenty fast because she wasn't about to make an extra effort for a . . . rodeo. Even if Westin Farr was there. He'd already been witness to her colossal fight with her brother, and that next morning when she was chased by the diabolical Maggie. Besides, she wasn't about to dress to impress. No . . .

When a honk sounded from the front of the house, she hurried out of her bedroom. It appeared she was the last one ready, and she squeezed into the back of the extended-cab truck between Glory and Pam.

"Well, look who decided to join us," Vonnie said. She wore a sequined turquoise top and a hat to match. It was really quite impressive. And loud.

Silvia suppressed a smile.

As Kellie drove away from the ranch, she expertly navigated the country roads until they got into town. Well, "town" was a relative word. Sure, there were a few shops—Mariah's Bakery, O'Malley's Shakes, a burger place called Scaggs, and a bar called Roosters—but the place was still tiny. They passed the bed and breakfast, then turned onto another road.

Up ahead, stadium lights blazed—well, rodeo arena lights.

Silvia was surprised at the number of cars and trucks parked in the dirt lot in front of the arena. It seemed this rodeo drew a decent-sized crowd.

"Wowie," Vonnie said. "I think all of Lost Creek is here, and the entire student body of Sam Houston."

"Rumor has it Knox Prosper is riding tonight," Kellie said. "He's going to give our boys a run."

"Who's Knox Prosper?" Silvia asked.

"One of the top bull riders in the country right now," Vonnie said. "And he's Kellie's cousin."

"Yep," Kellie said. "Although, I'll be cheering for Westin Farr over Knox." She shut off the engine, then opened her door.

After Silvia climbed out, she and Vonnie lagged behind the other women. "Does Kellie hate her cousin or something?" she asked Vonnie.

"Something like that." Vonnie toyed with her red braid that hung over one shoulder. "There was a family fallout, it seems. Knox used to be married to the woman who is now married to his brother, Holt."

"Wow." Silvia couldn't wrap her mind around that. "That sounds pretty... extreme."

"To say the least," Vonnie said.

"Do you think he'll win the bull riding?" Silvia wondered how good Westin was compared to Knox.

"There's a really good chance," Vonnie said. "Knox has been on a roll."

The women stood in line to get tickets, and Silvia checked out her surroundings. The bright lights, the booming music, the crowds, the boots, the hats . . . there was an energy about the place.

Once they got into the arena, Silvia sat with the group of women, even though her ticket put her somewhere in the front row. A guy dressed like a clown was standing in the middle of the arena, pretending to wrestle with a sheep. The crowd laughed at his antics.

Then the MC started up, welcoming everyone who'd traveled from out of town as well as the locals.

When he introduced the event riders, Silvia was pleased when she recognized the names of the cowboys who'd come to dinner at the ranch: Lars Jackson, Ford Hopkins, Reid Browning, Eric Davis, and Westin Farr.

She already knew that Ryan Prosper had retired from rodeo. And she couldn't deny the tiny flip in her chest when Westin's name was announced. She scanned the arena, looking for Westin, but when she didn't see him immediately, she refocused on the action in the arena. It seemed that bull riding would be the last event.

But Glory had been right. Silvia hadn't experienced a true rodeo until now, and the sheer rawness of the various events left her amazed and surprised at how much she enjoyed them. She gasped and cheered along with the crowd. She felt sorry for the calves in the calf roping, but the young animals seemed just fine after they'd been released from their ropes.

The team roping was fun to watch, and she didn't think she breathed at all during the barrel racing.

She didn't think anything could top the bareback riding that Reid Browning had done. His performance had made her stomach do a double-flip. He'd been declared the winner of the event, and the crowd had seemed pleased at that.

But when bull riders were announced, and the announcer added on the credentials of the bulls, Silvia's heart rate zoomed.

She leaned forward, gripping her hands together. It seemed the bulls' scores were just as important as the riders.

Westin would be the second-to-last rider, with Knox Prosper the last of the night. She glanced over at Kellie when Knox's name was mentioned. The woman had a placid expression on her face.

The seconds flew by with each bull rider. No one made it a full eight seconds—which, Glory informed her, was the minimum requirement. That, and the ride had to be aggressive and intense enough to get a judges' score. Eight seconds on a too-tame bull wasn't good enough.

"And heeeere we have Nitrous!" the announcer boomed. "A 1,600 pound bull with a 44.5 riding average. This is the first time our own Westin Farr has ridden this bull in competition."

Silvia's gaze flew to the bucking chutes, where she saw a man who had to be Westin. He wore a helmet and a thick vest. His shoulder worked as he adjusted his grip on the rope that circled the pale brown bull. The animal was already knocking against the metal gate, and the clanging could be heard in the arena.

Westin dipped his chin in a nod, and the gate flew open, pulled by another cowboy. Nitrous burst out of the gate like he was on fire. The music in the arena blared, thumping as hard as Silvia's heart. The bull leapt off the ground, arching high, then he twisted, and any normal human should have tumbled off.

But bull riders weren't normal humans.

Westin was hanging on tight, and even though he looked like he was in the middle of a Category 5 hurricane, he wasn't falling off.

Silvia hadn't even realized she was standing until the eight-second buzzer rang, and she jumped up and down with the cheering crowd. That bull was fierce enough to give Westin the top score.

Sure enough, the announcer said, "A score of 90.25! Westin Farr is currently in first place. With only one rider to go, we'll see who comes out on top tonight."

Silvia cheered with the others, although hers was more of relief now that Westin was jogging away from the still-furious beast. The clown distracted Nitrous from taking out his vengeance on Westin, and two other cowboys on horses maneuvered the bull through another gate then out of sight.

"And now, we have Duramax."

The black bull was huge.

"If this bull gives a good run, Knox will probably win," Vonnie muttered. "He's a higher-rated bull."

Silvia gripped Vonnie's hand as the black bull charged out of the gate, bucking, twisting, and all around trying to rid itself of the man on its back. Knox Prosper was good—very good. Even a newbie rodeo attendee like Silvia could see that. How in the world would a rodeo judge be able to decide between the two riders?

When the eight seconds were up, Knox Prosper landed solidly on the ground. He pulled off his helmet and waved it at the cheering crowd. His grin was wide, triumphant, as if he knew he'd won.

Silvia gripped Vonnie's hand tighter.

"Please let Westin win," she whispered to no one in particular.

Then Knox's score was read. And it took Silvia a second to realize it was a half-point lower than Westin's.

She screamed along with Vonnie and Glory. Then the three of them hugged each other.

Silvia was half laughing, half crying.

It was ridiculous. She'd met Westin Farr yesterday, and bull riding was his job. Just another night in a long string of them. But his victory felt like a victory for the whole ranch in some way.

If there weren't dozens of people and a series of fences blocking her path to Westin, she'd run down there and hug the man.

CHAPTER 12

SHE'D COME.

Westin had seen her walk in with the women from the recovery group right as the announcements began. Her black hat and red shirt made her like a beacon. A beautiful beacon.

Silvia Diaz looked fantastic in cowgirl apparel.

He wondered which woman he had to thank for that.

Westin had been to dozens—no, hundreds—of rodeos, so he wasn't missing out when he decided to watch Silvia instead. It was kind of like taking his nephew Jeppsen to one of those Disney movies. The kid's reactions were more entertaining to watch than the actual movie.

And it was the same with Silvia.

Westin chuckled at the way she became entranced by the events—wide-eyed and sometimes clapping and cheering. At one point, she covered her eyes with a hand—during the calf roping. It seemed she had a bit of a soft heart.

But when the bull riding started, he'd fully focused on his competition. He wasn't really worried about the other bull riders. Unless one of them had a fantastic night, and he didn't meet the eight seconds, then the only rider Westin had to worry about was Knox Prosper.

Over the last year, the guy had been solid. Pulling in top scores at most rodeos. Coming in second a time or two, but overall, he'd become the pro-leagues' darling. Tonight, Westin had to knock Knox out of that top spot.

When Westin found out he had Nitrous and Knox would be riding Duramax, that only made it more challenging. But Westin was up for the competition.

And now, as he walked back into the arena to wave at the cheering fans who'd just learned he'd won the bull riding event, his gaze again sought out Silvia's black hat and red shirt.

There she was, clapping and smiling.

He smiled back, but it was hard to tell if she knew the smile was directed toward her.

After accepting the cheers and applause, Westin jogged back to the fence and climbed over it. Hopping down on the other side, he was soon surrounded by other cowboys, including Knox Prosper.

"Well done, Farr," Knox said in that slow drawl of his. "I always say the best cowboy will always win, and you were the best tonight."

This was about the highest compliment a guy could get from someone like Knox.

"Thanks," Westin said. "Your ride was excellent."

Knox touched the brim of his hat in acknowledgment.

"Knox Prosper!" someone yelled, diverting his attention.

Knox gave another nod to Westin, then turned to talk to the young woman, who looked like she had more energy than a rabbit. She held out a piece of paper for his autograph.

"West! Nice job!" Reid and Eric had arrived.

"It was clutch, but you pulled it off." Reid had won his own rough stock event—bareback riding.

"You, too," Westin said. "I guess we've come a long way."

"True." Reid's brown eyes filled with amusement. The road to becoming successful at their events had taken years of hard work.

"I guess we're celebrating?" Eric said, clapping Westin on the shoulder. Eric had also won the tiedown roping tonight. "Meet at Roosters?"

"Are you going to YouTube us there?" Reid asked.

Westin laughed, since Eric had a YouTube series about ranching. And apparently, it was popular. Westin hadn't looked it up in a while, mostly because of the title—Rodeo King. Something he couldn't quite come to grips with and not laugh.

"Nah, bars are off limits," Eric said with a wink. "Anything that might involve alcohol and poor choices."

"Who's making poor choices?" Ryan asked, joining their group with Lars in tow.

"Nice job, man," Lars said, giving Westin a bro-hug.

"Thanks," Westin said.

"We're heading to Roosters," Eric said. "Bulldogger's treat."

"Why me?" Ryan said. "I've been feeding you yahoos all weekend."

Reid laughed. "We're all paying for ourselves. No debating."

Ryan looked relieved, and Westin grinned at the razzing going on with the guys. As fun as it was . . . his gaze kept straying to the crowd leaving the stadium. A line was forming of mostly cowgirls, waiting to congratulate the competitors.

The crowd was surprisingly thick, and as much as Westin tried to pay attention to where the women's recovery group was, he couldn't see them, or Silvia. They couldn't have gone far. If he didn't go search now, then he'd be caught up in the plans to head to the bar. And then what? The night would pass, and the sun would come up, and he'd be on his way to the airport.

And not see Silvia. For a week, if he was lucky, and if she left the ranch before he returned?

It wasn't like he could track her down in Seattle, could he?

Mind made up, he turned to Ryan. "Hey, I'll catch up with you guys later."

"Where you goin'?" Eric asked before Westin could slip away.

He paused. "I need to talk to someone."

"*Someone?*" Eric echoed, his tone suspicious and knowing at the same time.

"Do you mean Silvia Diaz?" Lars asked.

Westin stared at his friends. "How did you . . . Maybe. None of your business." He turned from them, because there were plenty of other people around who he didn't need knowing his business. He wasn't even ready to share it with his best friends. It was better to keep something like this private, especially when he didn't know what *this* was.

But getting out of the arena was a whole other matter entirely, when several people wanted to congratulate him. He tried to be as cordial and brief as possible.

When he arrived in the parking lot, he scanned for Kellie's truck—surely, the women had come in that.

But it was nowhere in sight.

Dang. Dang. Dang.

He released a half-growl, frustrated. He couldn't very well show up at the women's ranch at ten p.m. Except . . . He didn't have a way to contact Silvia now.

No cell number. No email. And he wasn't on social media like Eric was, so it wasn't like he could message her through Facebook or Instagram or whatever else there was.

Westin stared at the emptying parking lot, then he rubbed the back of his neck. His shoulder still ached, but he hadn't felt a thing during the ride. Not until now. Figured.

He was about to turn and head back to the guys when he heard someone say, "Hey, cowboy."

He spun to see Silvia Diaz leaning against the ticket booth. Her arms folded, her hat pulled low, her ankles crossed.

Westin's heart nearly stuttered to a stop. "Hey. I thought you left."

The edges of her lips curved up. "I'm supposed to be gone. Glory said she'd cover for me for a few minutes and use some excuse. We parked on the other side since we came late."

Westin walked toward Silvia. She didn't move. Only waited. Which was more than fine with him.

"Congratulations on your win," she said, her brown eyes moving up to meet his as he stopped in front of her.

"Thank you."

"That was some . . . ride." She unfolded her arms and tilted her head. "I mean . . . I've seen bull riding before, but I never knew anyone personally who does it. So I guess it seemed more intense."

Westin dipped his chin. "It is pretty intense."

Their eyes locked. Neither spoke for a heartbeat. Then two.

"Are you and the ladies going to Roosters?" he asked.

"No," she said. "Pam doesn't like crowds, and Glory says her bones are too old to dance. Emma was interested, but doesn't want to go alone."

Westin nodded. He was sort of glad Silvia wasn't going to the bar, either. Their gazes held again.

"I know you have a lot going on, Silvia," Westin said. Then stopped. Breathed. Started again. "But I wondered if I could get your number? I won't bother you too much. I promise. Maybe just a text here and there to check in. You know, see how you're doing."

She was watching him, and he didn't break his gaze. If there was one thing he wanted her to see in his eyes, it was his sincerity.

Her gaze seemed to warm to something positive. "Sure. Let me see your phone. Mine's back at the ranch."

He couldn't stop the grin on his face as he handed over his phone.

She added her contact, and he knew it was going to be hard to not pull it up immediately and text her.

When she handed it back, she said, "Well, I should get going. Congrats again."

He nodded, and she stepped past him.

"Silvia?"

She paused and turned.

"Thanks for waiting."

Her dark eyes warmed.

"Does this mean you're mooning over me?" he asked.

She laughed. "Don't push your luck, cowboy."

He loved her laugh, and he took a step closer. Would it be so bad to hug her goodbye?

But she inched away, her gaze coy. "Safe travels to Oklahoma."

"Right. And maybe I'll see you next weekend if you're still in Lost Creek."

"Maybe." She turned then, and he didn't call her back.

He didn't mind watching her walk away, though. Those boots did look fine on her.

"You comin'?" someone called out of a truck window.

It was Eric and Lars.

"Nah." Westin walked over to the truck. "Don't much like the crowds at the bar after a rodeo."

"That your honey?" Lars asked.

Westin frowned. "Who?"

"The woman in the black hat and red shirt," Eric asked.

Westin snapped his gaze to where he'd last seen Silvia, but she was long gone.

Both Eric and Lars laughed.

"That was Silvia, wasn't it?" Eric said. "The woman from the ranch—the one who made dinner tonight?"

"And you helped with it, according to the other ladies," Lars added.

Westin swallowed. "Yeah, it was Silvia. Hey, I gotta run. I'm heading out early for the airport."

"All right, man," Lars said. "Keep us posted on Silvia."

Westin smirked and shook his head as he strode off and headed to his truck.

He wouldn't be surprised if Eric or Lars posted something to The Chute. Secrets were never kept among the Six.

Sure enough, by the time he'd talked to a handful of people who offered more congratulations, and he climbed into his truck, texts from The Chute were already coming in.

But first, Westin opened the one from Silvia's brother. Axel had written: *Hey, man. Checking in. Hope things are well with you. Any news about my sister?*

Westin typed out a quick reply: *She went to the rodeo tonight with the women at the ranch. Dressed up in some cowgirl gear, too. Seemed to be enjoying her new friends.*

Ah, good to hear. Thanks, bro. Appreciate it.

Westin opened the group text next and began to read.

Ford: *You bailing on us, West?*

Eric: *He's got bigger and better plans tonight.*

Lars: *Yep, and her first name is Silvia.*

Ryan: *What are you guys talking about?*

Reid: *Are you serious, dog? How fast do you work, man? You just showed up yesterday.*

Ryan: *West, pick up your phone!*

Westin began to type quickly. *I'm leaving early for the airport. Nothing is going on with Silvia. I helped her make dinner. That's all. You can all go back to minding your own business now.*

Eric: *Did you get her number?*

Westin hesitated as the GIFs came through of hearts, and one of a kissing couple. *I got her number,* he finally wrote.

More GIFs of high-fives, fireworks, and one of a laughing puppy—what did that have to do with anything?

Westin's phone rang. It was Ryan.

"Yah?" he answered.

"What's going on, West?" Ryan asked. "Is Kellie going to be calling me with complaints?"

"No," Westin cut in. "Nothing's going on, I swear. I'm not interfering with any of the recovery activities."

"Cut the bull."

Westin sighed. "Fine. I like her. I helped make dinner after I got evicted from rodeo practice today. It was . . . nice. To be with someone who isn't off her rocker, you know?"

The guys all knew about the disaster that was Amy.

"Well, well . . ." Ryan murmured. "Does this have to do with who her brother is?"

Westin gave a surprised laugh. "Hardly. In fact, it's kind of a deterrent."

"What do you mean?"

"She has, uh, issues with him," Westin said. "Not that she's confided in me, but it's pretty clear."

"Ah." Ryan went silent.

"Recovery won't last forever, will it?" Westin said. "The women are there for what? A few weeks?"

Ryan sighed. "Yeah, it varies, though. I just know how much Amy has put you through the wringer."

At Westin's silence, Ryan said, "Is something going on there still?"

"She called me yesterday," he said. "Wants to get back together, which of course won't happen. But she's in my neighborhood, and that's why I'm going back home in the morning. Making sure she's not hanging around the family house."

Ryan whistled. "Do you think she'll go there?"

"My brain says no, but my gut is saying something else."

"Do you want me to come with you?"

It was a nice offer, and one that Westin wasn't surprised at. The Six always had his back. "I'll be fine."

"All right, keep me posted, though," Ryan said. "Oklahoma is only a plane flight away."

"Thanks, man," Westin said.

"And good luck with Silvia Diaz."

Westin released a breath. "This could all go south in a Texan second, you know. I mean, I got her number, but who knows if she'll even answer a text."

"Whatever happens, just be straight up with her," Ryan said. "If there's anything I've learned from my sister running the recovery program, it's that these women have been through tough stuff, and a lot of times, it comes from being lied to or manipulated by others."

Ryan was right.

And Westin could only hope Silvia would respond to a text from him—whenever it was she could respond.

After he hung up with Ryan, Westin started his truck. He headed to the bed and breakfast in town. He didn't want to be around the guys tonight or in the morning. So he needed a place to shower and get cleaned up. Besides, sleeping under his truck in the pasture was much too close to Kellie's ranch house—putting him in close proximity to Silvia Diaz.

And it was better, for both of them, that he give her as much space as possible.

For now.

CHAPTER 13

SILVIA HAD BEEN COOKING dinner for the past week. Apparently, her meal on rodeo night had been such a success that the women all voted Silvia in to be the designated dinner chef. Kellie had told Silvia she didn't need to cave to the peer pressure, but even her blue eyes had sparkled with hope.

Things could be worse. Silvia could be assigned one of the ranch chores, and if there was one thing she wasn't interested in, it was taking care of the horses. In any shape, activity, or form. She'd elected to skip out on the horseback riding excursions as well. Even though she was living in a house with six other women, she'd never had so much alone time in her life. As strange as it seemed.

She wasn't home, dealing with the rat race of school, dating, roommates, and family obligations.

She had hours sprinkled throughout the day where it was just her and her journaling. Or long walks through the fields. Or just hanging out on the front porch and watching the clouds move across the sky. When had she ever in her life had the time to do that?

Kellie had told her Axel called every day to check in.

Silvia still hadn't called him. She would, and she wanted to, eventually. But right now, it felt good to set this boundary. Putting her own emotional needs ahead of someone else's need to get information from her.

She'd talked to her mom a couple of times, albeit briefly.

Brighton had sent a few texts, but responding to her would be like responding to Axel.

Other than that . . . Silvia found that she loved cooking for a large group. She was also experimenting with different barbeque sauces and salsas. None of them had been rejected by her new female friends.

In fact, today, Kellie wanted to take her to Mariah's Bakery in town. Kellie said that everyone should have access to Silvia's fabulous barbeque sauce, so why not sell it at the bakery?

Silvia was flattered at the idea, but she wasn't going to be at the ranch for more than a couple of weeks at the most, so why bother?

Yeah . . . Silvia had decided to stay one more week.

And it had nothing to do with the fact that Westin Farr would be flying in tomorrow. He had another rodeo to go to the following day, but he'd be in Lost Creek in less than twenty-four hours. Not that Silvia was counting.

But they had been texting.

He'd kept to his promise and had only texted her a handful of times. To which she had to force herself not to reply right away.

Another text came through while she was waiting for Kellie on the porch.

Westin: *Good morning.*

She smiled, then wrote: *Good morning, how's Oklahoma?*

Pretty as a picture.

Send me one.

A picture?

Yes.

A few seconds later, a picture loaded—taking its time, of course—of a red barn and the field behind it.

Is that your house?

It's the barn behind my house.

I'm kidding, West. Yes, she was calling him West now.

Ah. The sarcasm didn't come through. Can we just talk on the phone and avoid all this confusion? Also, my fingers are tired.

She snickered. But her heart was also racing. Hearing his voice would . . . make this flirtation real. *Sorry, I'm heading into town with Kellie.*

Sounds fun.

She snickered again.

His next text came through. *Do you want to head into town tomorrow? Say, around noon? There's a café where a handsome bull rider will be having lunch.*

Ryan Prosper?

Her phone rang.

Westin was calling. Kellie would be out any second, and Silvia didn't really want to be talking to him when she stepped out on the porch.

Silvia's pulse was racing faster than it had on her morning run.

She rose from the porch and walked toward Kellie's truck, giving her some distance from the front door of the ranch. If the phone was still ringing when she got to the truck, maybe she'd answer. Just then, she remembered she'd turned off her voicemail since coming to the ranch. She didn't want any long-winded messages from her brother.

So . . . the phone was still ringing.

"You really have to stop calling so much," Silvia said into the phone. "I think I remember some sort of promise that if I gave you my number, you wouldn't pester me."

Westin's chuckle was low and deep, and a warm shiver caused goosebumps to rise on her arms.

"I was just making sure I have the right number," he drawled.

In person, his drawl hadn't seemed so heavy, but on the phone, it was more pronounced. She leaned against the truck, a smile growing on her face. "Well, who were you calling?"

"You."

Was it possible to blush from a single word? "I'm just glad to hear that you don't live in a barn."

He laughed. "That barn is in better shape than some people's houses. My dad was kind of a perfectionist."

"And your mom?"

"Chaos."

She laughed. "I guess opposites attract?" She sobered immediately. It was too late to take it back, though, and she didn't want him to think . . .

"I think I read that somewhere once," he said. "What are you doing in town today?"

Kellie still wasn't out yet—where was she?

Silvia hesitated. Anytime she'd ever told Axel anything about a plan or interest she had, he'd jump all over it. Take over. Make phone calls. Set things up. Move at warp speed when things were just a suggestion in her mind.

"Checking out the café for any bull riders?" he teased.

She smiled and told her mind to stop spinning. Westin wasn't Axel. At least, she hoped. "Actually, we're going to the bakery. Kellie thinks I should talk to the owner about selling my barbeque sauce at her place."

She waited. Held her breath, in fact.

"I guess I'm putting Lost Creek on my regular circuit now," he said. "If only to pick up a bottle of that ambrosia."

She smiled, feeling all warm and light inside. "Well, nothing's settled. I don't know if that's something I'd want to commit to, anyway. I mean, what am I supposed to do, ship bottles from Seattle?"

Here, Axel would have a business plan laid out in five seconds flat and be emailing distributors while still on the phone with her.

"You'll make the right decision," Westin said.

When had anyone ever said to her, *you'll make the right decision.* Never. If Westin were standing before her, she would be hugging him right now. Or maybe even kissing him. No. Just hugging. Still.

"But it will never change the fact that you make a helluva good sauce," he continued. "And if I remember right, your salsa was out of this world. Oh, and that guac. Wow, the best ever. Oh wait, that was *me.*"

She laughed.

The front door opened, and Silvia said, "Gotta go. Kellie's coming."

"Okay," he said. "And Silvia?"

She turned her back toward the approaching Kellie.

"Yeah?"

"Thanks for answering," he said, his voice low. "Even though it took you five rings."

"You're welcome."

His laugh was soft, and when she hung up, she was grinning. She tamped it down before Kellie reached her, and they climbed into the truck.

"How are you doing?" Kellie asked as she drove.

When Kellie asked that question, she was looking for much more than a "fine" answer.

"I'm reading that book on co-dependency and finding out that maybe my brother isn't the big, bad wolf."

Kellie smiled. "That book really changed the way I thought of my relationship with my ex-husband, too. I was so co-dependent on him that it made us both miserable."

Silvia was curious about this. Kellie didn't share a lot of personal experiences in group therapy. "I hope this isn't too intrusive, but when you divorced him, did that break the co-dependency?"

"Not even close," she said. "I mean, it was in my psyche, and I found that I was living my life co-dependent on others to affect my moods and determine my own value. I wasn't letting my higher power do his job."

It made perfect sense. Just because her brother made a suggestion or wanted to help her, didn't mean she had to accept his help. She could say, "No, thank you." At twenty-four years old, she hadn't mastered that simple concept. She hadn't set boundaries. She hadn't stood up for herself. She hadn't stuck to her own decisions.

"And now, you're not co-dependent on anyone?"

Kellie chuckled. "Let's just say I'm a work in progress. I'm not co-dependent on anyone for my self-confidence. But I'm still working on keeping my serenity intact. Especially last week."

"What happened last week?"

Kellie sighed. "My ex got remarried. To one of his *women.* Truthfully, I wish them all the best—especially her. She'll need it."

Silvia frowned. "Do you think he'll . . . uh, be unfaithful to her?"

"My first instinct is yes, but . . ." Kellie sighed. "Maybe she's the one for him, and they'll live happily ever after. Which, of course, means that I wasn't the one for him."

Silvia was surprised at the sad note in her voice. Even after all this time, did she still want her ex-husband back?

"What did I tell you?" Kellie said. "I'm still a work in progress. Running this recovery program has helped me on a personal basis. Listening to each of the women's comments and witnessing their growth and realizations only helps solidify mine."

Silvia nodded. "I've learned so much already."

"I'm glad you're staying another week," Kellie said.

"Me, too," Silvia said in a soft voice. "It might be longer. I'm kind of liking the person I'm turning into. It's like she's been there all along, though I've neglected her."

Kellie reached over and squeezed Silvia's hand. "You're an amazing person, Silvia. And once you figure that out, the world will have to watch out. But just remember, give yourself time to heal, and take one day at a time."

Silvia smiled, and her eyes filled with tears. Thinking about the future felt too overwhelming right now. Kellie was right, taking one day at a time, sometimes an hour at a time, was the best balm to preventing panic attacks. She'd even started an anxiety medication a couple of days ago. So far, so good, but she hadn't had any triggers, either.

When Kellie parked in front of Mariah's Bakery, Silvia's pulse began to race as she looked up at the green and white exterior of the café. This was getting real, and even though she didn't think anything would come of this introduction, she felt nervous all the same.

Kellie must have sensed her anxiety, because she said, "Mariah's a great lady. You'll love her, and if nothing else, we can get some pastries to take back to the ranch."

Silvia was never one to turn down pastries.

"Okay, then, let's go." Silvia popped open her door and climbed out of the truck. Then she walked with Kellie into the quaint shop. Green booths, white tables, and a cheerful atmosphere. The place smelled of all that one might expect from a bakery—warm, sugary, and like baking bread—so, heaven.

The display case had donuts, muffins, cookies, and pies.

But it was the menu that drew her attention. Soup in a bread bowl, chili and cornbread, tacos and quesadillas, barbeque plate lunches, chips and salsa and guac. Her mouth was already watering, and she wasn't even hungry.

The woman who came to greet them from behind the counter had to be Mariah. Her honey-brown hair was pulled into a ponytail, and she looked to be in her early thirties. She wiped her flour-specked hands on her apron, then extended her hand. "Nice to meet you, Silvia. I've heard a lot about you."

Silvia glanced at Kellie.

"We thought you might be interested in adding Silvia's creation to your menu," Kellie said, "but it will only make sense if the two of you agree."

Mariah nodded. "Let's see what you've got."

Kellie produced the sack that apparently Silvia had forgotten to grab from the kitchen counter at the ranch. It contained three bottles of sauce that she'd made the night before. Overnight marinating would make them robust with flavor by now.

"Great." Mariah took the bottles out of the bag and set them on the counter. "Let me grab some chicken that's ready to be served. We can all have some. In fact . . ." She headed over to one of the occupied tables, where a cowboy who looked older than the town of Lost Creek sat with a girl of about ten, who must be his granddaughter.

"Charlie, do you and Sherry want to be part of our taste test?"

Charlie's gaze shifted toward Silvia, then back to Mariah. "Sure thing. I'll eat anything made by a pretty lady."

Mariah laughed. "Be careful what you wish for."

Charlie's wrinkles creased even further with his smile.

"What is it?" Sherry asked, her young voice eager and curious.

"We're testing out a new barbeque sauce on chicken," Mariah said with a wink. "I hope you're both hungry."

It appeared they'd had milkshakes, but no food.

Mariah drew a second table near Charlie's, then she bustled into the back kitchen and returned with a pan of grilled chicken strips and a stack of small plates.

"Everyone take a plate," she instructed.

Silvia did as well, although she didn't really need to taste test. She was more interested in the reactions of Mariah, Charlie, and his granddaughter.

Everyone began to eat, and to Silvia's surprise, Charlie didn't say a word as he ate several bites. After a few moments, he folded his aged hands atop the table, and looked at her with his blue-gray eyes. "Ma'am, this is the best barbeque I've ever tasted. And I've been on this earth for a long, long time. In my opinion, if Mariah here decides to carry it, she'll have folks coming from miles away, and the line will be out the door."

Silvia blinked back the threatening tears in her eyes and released a breath. "Thank you, sir," she managed to say over a tightening throat.

"I agree," Mariah said, her smile wide. "What do you think, Silvia? Ready to do business with me?"

CHAPTER 14

WESTIN HAD HOPED IT wouldn't come to this, but Amy had lied to him.

She'd told him she'd left town when he reached out to her the moment he arrived at his mom's place. But when he'd gone to the grocery store, the store manager, Bill, had told him Amy had been there multiple times, asking if Westin was in town yet.

Westin had made it no secret that he and Amy were over, and living in a small town, even Bill knew about it. That's when Westin had decided to check the security footage of his mom's place. Amy had been to the house every day, multiple times, different hours. Her bleached-blonde hair was a dead giveaway.

Seeing the footage had pushed him to call Kellie Prosper and ask for advice. Since she was in the wellness and therapy industry, maybe she'd have some suggestion of how he could help Amy. Yeah, he could file a restraining order, but he was sure there were other ways. Better ways.

So, here Westin sat, waiting for Amy to show up at the pancake house.

Maybe he shouldn't have invited her for a meal. After all, he didn't want her to read into it, but he also had to make a few things clear.

When the door next opened, the hairs on the back of his neck stood, and he looked up to see Amy walking in.

She'd grown thinner. Amy had always been slender, but now she looked . . . too thin. Not healthy. Her clothing was baggy and too heavy for the warm, sunny day outside. Her black leggings were paired with a long-sleeved shirt, and she wore a beanie cap as if they lived in Alaska or something.

The compassion inside Westin stirred, but he had to remain strong.

Her gaze found him, and she didn't smile, but wore a look of triumph on her narrow features that he'd seen before, when he'd called things off. It was like she didn't believe he was serious.

Well, she was about to find out otherwise.

She slipped in the booth on the other side of him, then reached for his hand. A move that was familiar to him, but one that wouldn't happen now.

He drew back.

She narrowed her eyes. "I don't have cooties, Westin."

"That's not what this is about," he said. "Do you want to talk first, or order first?"

"I'm not hungry," she shot back. Folding her arms, she added, "Nice that you pick a public restaurant. Afraid of what I might say?"

"No." Westin picked up his phone and showed her a series of screenshots from the security camera footage. The security system was perhaps the best investment he'd ever made.

As he scrolled through the pictures, Amy's face paled.

"What? You think that's me?" she asked.

"I have no doubt it's you," Westin deadpanned.

"Well, you can't prove it," she said in a tight voice.

"I think I can," he said. "The technology will match you to any picture I might have of you."

Her gaze leveled with his, but he didn't back down, didn't look away.

"I've committed no crime," she said. "I was just seeing if you were home. Had to walk a little to stretch my legs."

"You knocked on the front door, then went around to the back of the house," Westin said in a perfectly calm voice. "You tried the back door, found it locked, then tried to open a window." He showed her more pictures.

This time, her gaze did drop, and she began to tug at the hem of her long-sleeved shirt. He could guess why she was dressed this way on a too-warm day.

"If you're not hungry, then you might as well meet a friend of mine."

Her eyes widened at this, and grew even wider when a dark-haired woman in a navy skirt and pink blouse strode up to the table.

"Amy?" she said. "I'm Ellie. I'm with Bethany's Place—a women's rehabilitation facility."

Amy's face pinked, and she gaped at Westin. "You staged an *intervention*?"

Westin raised his hands. "Look, just hear her out." He scooted over in the booth, and Ellie sat next to him.

She began to talk, telling Amy about the program that could help women get through tough situations. "We not only support you through recovery, but our group helps you transition as well. Find employment or get an education—"

Amy stood abruptly, her sharp gaze still on Westin. "I can't believe you did this," she hissed. "I'm not a junkie. We're over. *Really* over!"

"Amy." Ellie stood as well and reached a hand out to her.

But Amy backed away, her spiteful gaze now on Ellie. "Leave me alone. I'm fine. I don't need anyone."

"Amy," Westin said in a quiet voice. People in the restaurant were looking over at them now. He didn't care, but he didn't want anything to cause Amy to...

Too late. She turned and hurried out of the restaurant.

Westin moved out of the booth, but Ellie put a hand on his arm. "Let her go."

"We surprised her, that's all," he said. "I know she needs help, and—"

"This was a good first step," Ellie said, her hazel eyes focusing on him. "She knows that *you* know. Even if she won't admit it to you or anyone else. Someday, she'll understand you brought me in because you care about her."

"But she left," Westin said. "What if she uses because she's upset?"

"We can't live our lives asking, 'what if,'" Ellie said in a gentle tone. "She'll make her choices, and when she hits rock bottom, she'll find help. Maybe it will be through me, or through someone else."

Westin blinked hard. He was battling between running after Amy and staying to listen to Ellie.

"But *she* has to want it, Westin," Ellie continued. "What you did today was great. It was important, and now, you need to let her go."

Westin frowned. "We're broken up—have been for months. I don't even think of her in that way anymore."

Ellie gave a patient smile. "You're still feeling responsible for her. Co-dependent, if you will. That's why you called me, and that's great. I'm glad you did. But unless you can be a supportive friend to her, and not give her hope of a future relationship, you need to cut ties."

Westin rubbed the back of his neck and blew out a breath. "I'm not interested in dating her. We're not a match, and I should have never dated her in the first place."

"Okay, then." Ellie squeezed his arm. "You have your answer, then. Keep in touch, and I'll let you know if she reaches out to me. Just so you can rest easy about it."

"She didn't seem too excited to talk to you, so what makes you think she'll reach out?"

Ellie gave a soft laugh. "I slipped a card into her handbag with a pack of cigarettes. She'll find it soon enough."

Westin nodded. He felt better, but only marginally. Was what Ellie said true? That he hadn't really let go of Amy? Of course, he had. Yet, he'd answered her phone calls. He'd come back to Oklahoma intent on talking to her. He'd staged an intervention.

"I'm a mess," he murmured.

Ellie tilted her head. "You're doing what's right. You tried to help a friend. Now, it's up to her."

"All right." Westin shoved his hands into his pockets, looking over at the restaurant door again. Amy was long gone. He should be grateful, but there was still a knot in his stomach. A knot of worry.

Once he said goodbye to Ellie and thanked her, he headed outside to his dad's old ranch truck he'd driven over to the restaurant. A text from Axel had come in while he'd been in the restaurant.

Checking in again. How's it all going? Heard anything from Silvia lately?

Westin typed out a quick reply. *Still in Oklahoma, but heading to Lost Creek tomorrow. If I see her, I'll let you know how she's doing.* He left out the detail that he was definitely planning on seeing her, and they'd been texting all week.

Sounds good, Axel wrote. *Thanks so much.*

Westin had one more night at the house, then he'd be heading back to Texas. Since his mom was still staying at his sister's, he called Cheryl and updated her about Amy.

"You did the right thing, West," she said. "You can't save everyone, you know. And Ellie was right, Amy needs to decide she wants to get clean on her own. Or rehab will be a waste."

"Yeah, that's what I'm learning," Westin said as he started up the old truck. The engine rumbled to life.

"You in Dad's truck?" Cheryl asked.

He chuckled. "Yeah, how did you guess?"

"It's louder than ever!"

Westin was still smiling when he hung up with his sister. He made the drive home, no radio, no distractions. Just a quiet country road to give him a lot of thinking time.

When he stopped in front of the house, he turned off the engine, but remained in the truck. Thinking. He was definitely over Amy. But Ellie had been right. He'd felt compelled to help her, to make sure their breakup didn't push her off any edges. He didn't know the extent of the addictions she might be battling, but he hoped Ellie was right about Amy changing her mind.

Westin exhaled slowly, then he pulled his phone out again.

He read through the texts from The Chute, and replied to a couple of the teasing comments on there. The guys were razzing each other about their upcoming rodeo events. Sometimes, Westin wondered if Ryan was bothered by all their rodeo talk—since he couldn't ride anymore—but he always dished out his own teasing.

Then a text came in from Silvia.

Westin's skin warmed as he clicked over to it. Before he knew it, he was grinning. Silvia had been flirty this past week, but she always seemed to be holding back. Which, he knew, wasn't in her character. She had no problem stating her opinion or pushing when she didn't agree with something.

With him, though . . . sometimes, she was downright reserved. Or maybe it was careful?

Hey, so Mariah wants my barbeque sauce. A week's supply. Where's my kitchen helper when I need him?

Westin couldn't let this text be answered by another text. He hoped she could answer the phone, because he was calling her.

Four rings later, Silvia said in a hushed tone, "Hello?"

"Congratulations, darlin'." The endearment had just slipped out.

"Thanks, I'm kind of in shock."

"I'm not surprised at all," he said. "In fact, if Mariah had turned you down, I would've had a word with her."

Silvia laughed. "You wouldn't dare."

"I would."

She snickered. "Whatever. Why can't I hang around men who are less like cavemen? Always speaking up for their women."

The silence between them warmed.

"Um, that came out totally wrong," she said in a fierce whisper. "And I can't really talk right now. Too many people around, if you know what I mean."

"Do you really think I'm a caveman?" Westin asked. Would that explain him trying to help Amy when she didn't want it?

"Too soon to know," Silvia said. "Look, I'm hanging up now."

"Okay, okay. Congrats, Silvia, that's amazing. You're amazing."

She didn't answer, but he knew she was still there.

"That didn't come out wrong, if you're wondering."

"I wasn't wondering, I was . . . Oh, never mind. See you later, West."

Then she hung up. Just like that.

She was busy, he got that. She was with the others at the ranch, he got that, too. But he wished he could talk to her in person. Right now. Their conversation over the phone seemed to have been going somewhere, even though he wasn't sure where exactly.

She'd called him a caveman jokingly, but she'd also said, "Always speaking up for their women." . . . Did that mean she considered him relationship potential?

Westin had no problem with that. Yeah, there were complications with that—a lot, namely that they lived in two opposite locations. But *Silvia Diaz.* He closed his eyes. She was funny, spunky, feisty, passionate, a dang good cook, lovely to look at, and he couldn't stop thinking about her.

CHAPTER 15

SILVIA CALLED HER BROTHER.

It was time.

And she knew enough to call him in the morning, since he was scheduled to play later tonight. So he'd be in his hotel room by himself before breakfast.

Axel answered on the first ring. "Silvia. How are you? Is everything okay?"

Silvia wasn't going to lie, it was good to hear his voice. So maybe she missed him, but that didn't mean there weren't a lot of things to iron out in their relationship.

"Everything is fine," she said, pacing her small bedroom. Her nerves were a jumble. "I'm staying another week."

The relief in Axel's sigh was plain. "That's great, Silv, really great. Kellie told me you're doing well. I can't ask for anything more. No panic attacks there, right?"

Silvia released her own sigh. "That's not my biggest problem, Axel." She took a deep breath, because this was going to be hard, but it needed to happen. "In fact, I'll probably deal with them the rest of my life when I hit overload. I called you because I need you to stop hovering. I need you to let me make my own decisions. I need you to just be a brother. Not a father."

"Silv, I'm not—"

"And I need you to listen to me right now," she cut in. "You can't tell me how I feel. You're not me. I'm telling you how *I* feel right now, and you're not going to be able to change that or fix that. Bottom line is that I need space. Both at this ranch and when I leave here. I'm going to text you a couple titles of books I want you to read. When you've read them, we can talk again."

She could practically feel Axel's surprise through the phone. She'd never, ever been this blunt with him. "And Axe, thank you for always taking care of me and Mom. I'll always be grateful, and I love that you're my brother. There are some things we need to work on, and one of those is to stop being co-dependent."

"Co-dependent?" he asked. "What do you mean by that?"

His voice wasn't exactly hostile, but it wasn't enthused, either.

"I'll text you the name of the book about it," she said. "Text me when you've read both of what I'm sending you."

"All right, I'll read them," Axel said. "I only want you to be happy, sis. You know that. Everything I've done for you is because I love you—"

"I know that, but we need a more healthy love," Silvia said. "I need to go now. We need to both be coming from the same place—which will happen when you read those books."

"All right," Axel said, his voice quiet now.

She closed her eyes, feeling like she'd had some sort of victory, but also feeling exhausted with the emotion that had built up to it.

"I'm so proud of you, Silv," he said.

She blinked back the tears stinging her eyes. "We'll talk soon, okay?"

"Okay."

When Silvia hung up with her brother, she sat on the bed in her small bedroom. Her hands were shaking as she texted him the two book titles. One was about family systems, and the other about co-dependency. They'd both opened her eyes and taught her so much already.

She should send them to her mom, too, but something stopped her. It was like she didn't want her mom's happy bubble to be popped. Her mom was an angel, and she lived her life serving others. No faults in that. Yet, Silvia had learned to keep her resentments buried because of her mom's example. Maybe there would be a time and place to share these deeper things with Mom.

But Silvia had to deal with first things first, which had been her brother.

She checked the time. Westin wouldn't be flying for a couple of hours, not that she was counting down. Surprisingly, she was looking forward to seeing him. When she shouldn't. She had no business flirting with a cowboy from Oklahoma who spent most of his time driving a beat-up truck to rodeo arenas, then proceeded to torture his body atop a raging bull.

The whole time he'd been in Oklahoma this week, he hadn't mentioned his ex-girlfriend once. Silvia admitted she was curious—had he seen her? Had they talked? Was he considering getting back together?

All of his calls and texts had been getting more and more flirty. But maybe that was her imagination, and she was reading into things that weren't there. Maybe all guys in Oklahoma were like Westin. Polite, charming, heart on their sleeves . . .

Silvia sighed. She couldn't sit on her bed all morning, even though Saturdays had a lighter agenda. She planned to make more batches of barbeque sauce and deliver it to

Mariah's. The sauce wasn't due until Monday, but what if... What if Westin wanted to hang out with her?

Not like a date. Maybe a drive. And not what he'd suggested—taking her out on some horses. No thanks.

Silvia stood and set her phone aside. Then she headed into the kitchen. The coffee machine was brewing, and Kellie sat at the table with some tea. Silvia knew it was orange tea, which she'd started drinking it herself.

"Good morning," Kellie said, smiling, her blue eyes warm. Her blonde hair was pulled into a messy bun.

"Good morning." Silvia opened a cupboard and fetched a mug, then filled it with water from the sink. Next, she put it in the microwave to heat it up. "You'll be relieved to know I talked to my brother this morning."

"How did it go?"

"Fine," Silvia said, then smirked. "Gave him some homework."

Kellie chuckled. "Good for you."

Silvia nodded, warmth blooming in her chest. The microwave dinged, and she took out the steaming mug. Then she dunked a tea bag into it and anchored it with a teaspoon.

Next, she took a seat across from Kellie while waiting for the tea to steep.

"How are you doing?" she asked Kellie.

The woman's brow wrinkled. "Fine."

"Women say that a lot, don't we?"

"That's the truth," Kellie said on a sigh. "You know, I'm not fine. Hardly slept last night. It appears my ex-husband is claiming I stole money from him during our marriage. I didn't, of course, but now we're getting lawyers involved again."

"What a creep," Silvia said, then clamped her hand over her mouth. "Sorry. Was that cross talking?"

Kellie laughed so hard, she had to wipe her eyes. "Oh, gosh, I needed that. Thanks, Silvia. And no, we can talk like normal people in the kitchen." She was still chuckling as she reached for her mug.

"Glad I could help."

Kellie winked, then she sobered. "By the way, Ryan told me Westin is staying at his place this weekend..."

Silvia didn't meet the woman's eyes as she stirred the teabag in her own mug.

"Do you know anything about that?"

Silvia glanced up. "About Westin? Or about Ryan?"

"I don't want to get in the middle of anyone's business," Kellie said in a careful tone. "But Westin and my brother go way back. He's like a brother to me, too. And you're a beautiful woman, Silvia, so I'm not surprised Westin is interested. I just... I don't want him to get hurt. You live in Seattle, and—"

Kellie didn't need to finish. Silvia knew exactly what was going on. "My brother told you about the men I've dated, didn't he?"

"He had concerns about your past behavior," she said. "Your impulsiveness and how you date guys for a few weeks at a time, then dump them, only to be dating another guy soon after."

Silvia took a sip of her tea, even though it was too hot. She could feel her temper rising, and that wasn't a good thing. She focused on taking a steadying breath. "My brother is overprotective, and like I said in group, way too co-dependent."

"I totally get that, I really do," Kellie said. "I don't mean to offend you. But if you're not interested in Westin as much as he's interested in you—according to Ryan—can you make sure that's clear?"

First, Silvia wondered what in the world Westin had said

to Ryan about her. He'd been in Oklahoma hanging out with his ex-girlfriend, for heck's sake. Second, Axel had seriously crossed the line. But she'd have to deal with that later. Right now, Kellie Prosper was looking for an answer, and Silvia didn't know if she had one.

She stared down at the mug in front of her. The orange scent was sweet, calming, but that didn't slow down her pulse any.

"Here's the thing, Kellie," Silvia said in a quiet voice as she lifted her gaze. "I've done a lot of dumb things, and only a single week here has made that clear. But I've also learned to own my decisions and to realize that the sum of my mistakes and successes are part of my journey in life. It's what makes me grow."

Kellie nodded, but didn't respond.

"So," Silvia continued, "if I were to tell you the absolute truth, it would be that I like Westin. We live in different states, and heaven knows, we're pretty much opposites. But we have things in common, too. Deeper things. I can't really explain it. While I'd love to tell you I'm not going to spend time with Westin, that isn't true. If he invites me somewhere, I'm going to say yes. And if things move forward from there, I'm going to see where it leads." She took a breath. "Westin can make up his own mind about me, although I'm sure he appreciates his friends' concern."

Kellie tapped a finger against her lips. "That's just it. He doesn't appreciate our concern. According to Ryan, he told the rodeo guys to mind their own damn business."

Silvia had to try really hard to hold back a smile. If Westin walked into the kitchen right now, she'd jump up from the table and kiss him. "He *said* that?"

"Yeah," Kellie said. "And that's not the Westin I know. He's an open book. He's a kind soul, an old soul."

Silvia knew this even after such a short time. "I'm not interested in changing him, Kellie. But I will say that I agree with him."

It took Kellie a moment to respond. "All right, then, just let me know if you're going off property. If I'm not around, leave a note so we aren't expecting you for something."

Silvia wanted to cheer. Instead, she gave a regal nod. "Fair enough."

"Well, look who's already up," Glory said, coming into the kitchen in her giant pink bathrobe. "Coffee's on. How could I resist that?"

"Help yourself," Kellie said. "I'm heading into town to get a few supplies for the rest of the weekend. Anyone want to join me?" She looked pointedly at Silvia.

But in Silvia's opinion, she'd said her piece. "I'm going to work on the batches of barbeque sauce that I promised Mariah."

"Ooo," Glory said. "In that case, I'll get out of your way after I eat."

Silvia smiled. "That was smooth."

Glory only winked, then she turned to the cupboard to fetch a mug.

The morning passed both quickly and slowly. Quickly, because Silvia stayed busy making multiple batches, and slowly, because she kept checking the time. Westin hadn't texted at all. Did that mean he'd landed? Was he driving? Did he decide to skip Lost Creek altogether and head to the rodeo grounds where he'd be riding tonight?

Silvia turned on the radio to distract herself from her own cycling thoughts.

The women came and went. Lunch was on everyone's own time, so nothing was formal. At one point, Silvia made more tea, but she was more focused on pouring the barbeque sauce into the bottles that Mariah had sent home with her, along with labels.

The woman had ordered more bottles and labels that would be showing up next week. Silvia had told Mariah not to order too many since she didn't know how long she'd be at the ranch, but Mariah had assured her that everything was returnable.

It was nearly two when Silvia had all the bottles lined up and ready to go. She only had to box them, then load them into Kellie's truck—Kellie had said she'd be ready anytime. All Silvia had to do was holler.

She was taking a moment to admire her handiwork and enjoy the rush of accomplishment it gave her when her cell phone chimed. For some unexplained reason, Silvia's heart leapt. She looked at her phone. *Westin.*

She wiped her hands on her apron and opened the text.

What's a cowboy gotta do to get someone to answer the front door of the ladies' ranch?

"He's here," Silvia breathed. Then she hurried through the kitchen to the front door and swung it open. She probably looked like she'd been in the kitchen all day, which she had, but she didn't care.

Westin Farr stood on the front porch, his hat in hand. Nothing was shading his green eyes now, and they seemed lighter than she remembered. Had it only been a week since she'd seen him? It felt much, much longer.

When she'd first met Westin, as out-of-sorts as she was, she'd appreciated his good looks. But now . . . he was absolutely delicious. He'd shaved, that much was clear. And his hair was mussed on top, indicating he'd had his hat on all day—of course. She wouldn't mind mussing it up more.

And his smile . . . it sent little zaps of heat to her toes.

"Is everyone asleep or something?" he asked.

Swoon. His voice was so much better in person. Everything about Westin was much better in person.

"I have no idea," Silvia said. "I must not have heard your knock. I had the radio on in the kitchen."

Westin leaned against the door frame, his gaze slowly scanning her face. She caught his scent now. Soap and leather. It did something funny to her pulse.

"Ah, I thought I was banned," he said. "I didn't want Kellie to catch me trying to come in the back door."

Silvia smiled at this. "We definitely wouldn't want that." She was studying him right back. Something had changed between them. She couldn't name it, but it was there. "Want to come in? I'm just getting ready to load up my batches of sauce."

"I can help," he said immediately.

Silvia laughed, then she stepped back, allowing him to enter. He walked past her, and again she caught his scent. She followed him into the kitchen, and she may or may not have checked him out from behind.

"Holy guacamole," Westin said, then added a low whistle.

"Did you just say, 'holy guacamole?'"

He flashed her a grin, and a few things inside of her melted.

"This is amazing, darlin', I mean truly incredible." He circled the table, turning some of the bottles.

He'd called her darlin' the day before on the phone, but she hadn't allowed herself to absorb it, to think anything of it. He was a cowboy. They talked like that. But here, in this small space of a kitchen, and with his green eyes on her—it felt personal.

More parts inside of her melted.

"How are you hauling all these bottles?"

Silvia pointed to the boxes stacked in the corner. "Loading them in those boxes, then Kellie said she'd drive me into town."

"I can take you," he said, his voice low, his gaze steady.

It only took her a heartbeat to decide. "All right."

CHAPTER 16

HOW DID A COWBOY go about asking a girl on a date? One that would consist of driving two hours, then sitting in a rodeo arena by herself, followed by another two hour drive back. Would she be bored to tears? Be impatient? Put out that it wasn't a fancy dinner and a movie?

Silvia Diaz was still a mystery to Westin, and he was sure she'd been wooed plenty of times. The problem was, he was a simple guy.

They'd delivered the cases of barbeque sauce, and Westin had even been able to try some when he told Mariah he hadn't eaten all day.

She'd sat them both down and insisted on bringing them complimentary chicken lunches, with Silvia's amazing sauce, of course.

Silvia had acted surprised, uncomfortable, and unusually quiet. This stumped Westin. She was outgoing, outspoken, but in the café, she'd been so quiet.

Now, as they drove back to the ranch, Westin glanced over at Silvia's profile. She'd braided her hair today, and wisps had escaped, curling against her face. She was currently biting her lip and gazing out the passenger window.

"What's going on in that pretty head of yours?" he asked.

She looked over at him, startled, as if she'd forgotten he was even there. "I, uh, it's dumb."

Westin smiled. "I doubt it's dumb. You look like you have the weight of the world on your shoulders."

She looked down at her hands, which she'd clamped tight. "It's just that . . . I hate to let Mariah down. She's so excited about the barbeque sauce, but what if customers don't like it? Besides, I'm not going to be at the ranch much longer, and I don't want to flake out if they *do* like it. It's not like I can make it and ship from Seattle. That would cut out all profit and defeat the purpose. Not that I'm desperate for money, because my brother pays for stuff still, although I don't want him to anymore, you know."

She looked over at him, and he nodded to show he was listening.

"My brother always wants to take care of everything, provide everything, but I've realized that I'm letting it control me." She closed her eyes for a second. "I love him, but I didn't even tell him about this barbeque sauce thing because he'd leap into action. Call more restaurants. Ask one of his contacts to design a label. And I . . . I just want to do this on my own. Fail on my own, maybe. Or succeed. I don't even care. It just has to be *me*."

Another glance.

Her tone was sounding panicked, and he didn't like that one bit. She should be proud of herself. She should be thrilled that Mariah was putting in orders. She should know that no one was going to hate her creations.

"I probably sound stupid and ungrateful," she continued. "I've only talked to him once since I've been here—and it was this morning. I basically told him he had to read two books before I'd talk to him again. And he's a busy man. He's married, you know. And he's got my mom to worry about, too. He's on the road this week, playing in different states, being the superhero shortstop of the MLB. Yet, he's calling Kellie every day, asking about *me.* Worrying about me—his sister who's accomplished nothing in her life."

Westin slowed the truck and parked beneath a group of trees a few feet off the road.

"What are you doing?" Silvia said, her gaze taking in their surroundings.

"Let's go for a walk," he said.

Silvia frowned. "Where are we?"

"About a half-mile from the ranch. There's a little stream through those trees, and it's a nice place to visit. We call it boulder stream, since there are boulders on each side."

Her expression was dubious, and she was still sitting in the truck by the time he got out and walked around to the passenger side. So he opened her door and held out his hand.

She looked at his hand, then met his gaze. "I'm fine."

"I know you're fine," he said, keeping his hand extended. "Want to take a walk anyway?"

She sighed and took his hand. He helped her down, then didn't let go. She didn't pull away, either.

Fine with him. He led her past the trees where he'd parked, then along a path that cut through some brush until it opened up to the stream he'd told her about. A few trees grew close to the bank, providing a nice spot of shade.

He walked with her over to the boulder, where they sat together, Westin a little behind her.

She pulled up her knees and rested her chin on them as she gazed at the ambling water.

He waited, and waited some more. He really didn't mind.

There was plenty of time before the rodeo, and as far as he was concerned, Silvia needed some time to work out her own thoughts.

When she finally sighed and looked over at him, he didn't know what to expect her to say, but it wasn't, "How did you know?"

"How did I know what?"

"That I was freaking out?" Her voice trembled.

"Hey," he said, moving forward so they were right next to each other. "You're not freaking out. You're just in a new place, a new situation. You have lots to think about and consider."

She took a shaky breath and wiped at her fallen tears.

He slipped an arm around her, and she leaned into him. He loved that she smelled like barbeque sauce and spice and the strawberry soda she'd had at the café.

"I have panic attacks, you know," she whispered.

He nodded.

She lifted her head and looked at him. "Did you know?"

"No, but I'm sorry you do. My sister has them sometimes."

"She does?" Surprise shone in her beautiful brown eyes. "What does she do to get rid of them?"

"She sits by a stream with a handsome cowboy."

When Silvia smiled, Westin knew he'd said something right. And he knew that Silvia Diaz would be a really easy person to fall in love with.

"You're kind of amazing, Westin Farr."

His heart thumped hard. "You shouldn't say stuff like that. It's going to go to my big head."

She turned so she was facing him more, then she reached up and tugged off his hat. "It's not that big."

Westin laughed. "I'll let the others know. Ryan will be right pleased to know that I'm salvageable after all."

Silvia's smile was soft, and her direct gaze was making his skin heat up more than it already was. She'd stopped crying, and for that he was grateful. And the shade wasn't doing a darn thing to cool him down. Maybe he should wade into the stream to get some sense back into him.

"How are you feeling now, darlin'?"

She inhaled a steady breath, then released it. "Better, actually. Thank you."

"I did nothing." His hand reached for hers. "But I'm glad you're feeling better. Takes time, that's all. My sister told me that."

Silvia nodded, then she tilted her head and gave him a small smile. The sunlight sprinkled through the trees above, landing on her pretty face, and making her hair look as smooth as a river rock. Her brown eyes weren't worried or panicked anymore, and the warmth in them seemed to reach into his heart and heat up all kinds of things in his body. He hoped to heaven she couldn't read his thoughts, because they weren't very pure right now.

"You know, I've never been kissed by a bull rider."

Westin was sure he'd stopped breathing. Was she saying . . . was she *asking*? "I could rectify that, darlin'," he said over the pebbles in his throat.

When those eyelashes of hers fluttered closed, he did what any gentleman would do with such a request from a pretty woman. He leaned close and kissed her.

Silvia Diaz tasted like strawberry soda.

And heaven.

He braced one hand on the boulder, and the other he slipped behind her neck. Silvia's hands moved across his chest, then over his shoulders. As she pressed closer, he'd bet money that she could feel his heart thundering, if not hear it loud and clear.

Westin had kissed his share of women, but he wouldn't put Silvia into that category. She wasn't simply a woman, she was someone who'd somehow gotten ahold of his heart. And he didn't mind. Not one bit.

Silvia's mouth was warm and welcoming against his, and he deepened his kiss, testing, tasting.

She only tugged him closer, and he smiled, moving his hand down her back and settling at her hip. He was quickly lost in her taste and touch. There was no going back now.

The sounds of the stream and the breeze surrounded them, and Westin couldn't think of a better way to pass a Texan afternoon.

"West," Silvia breathed, pulling away for a moment.

Her brown eyes seemed to implore him, and he wasn't sure what she wanted, what she needed.

"I'm . . . I'm glad I met you," she said.

His heart raced for a different reason. Maybe she was trying to let him down easy? "I'm glad I met you, too, darlin'. Are you regretting this?" He had to ask, had to know. The sooner, the better.

Her brow lifted. "No, are you?"

He scanned her beautiful face. And couldn't think of one reason why he'd regret kissing Silvia. "Not at all."

She smiled. "Me, neither."

"So you don't want a recall?"

She laughed.

He loved her laugh. It was prettier than the musical stream.

"I want to see you ride tonight," she said, her voice coy and light. But her fingers were tracing the back of his neck, distracting him quite thoroughly.

"It's a long drive to Mount Palmer."

"I'm not busy."

"It's a deal, and I think we should seal it." He tugged her onto his lap and kissed her again. It was a nice thing to discover that she fit against him perfectly. He decided he wasn't going to let go of her anytime soon, and she seemed more than fine with that.

Chapter 17

If anyone would have told Silvia two weeks ago that she'd be at a rodeo, standing and cheering for a bull rider who was hanging on with all the grit a person could muster to not be thrown by a bull named Red Rosy, she would have never believed it.

Yet, here she was. The night was perfect. Not too hot or too cool. The stands were nearly full, and Silvia was wedged between an older man who had enough tobacco in his cheek to share with the entire row, and a woman who had likely used a full can of hairspray on her updo.

Silvia wore the same black hat and boots from the weekend before, borrowed again from Glory. If Silvia was going to make this a habit, she needed to go shopping at one of those ranch stores.

Meanwhile, the eight-second buzzer sounded, and the crowd erupted into cheers. Those who weren't already on their feet were standing now. Westin was clearly in the lead—he had to be. Even a newbie like Silvia could see the intensity of the ride and how Red Rosy hadn't let up for even a second.

She exhaled in relief when Westin was over the gate, safe

from the raging bull who was looking for revenge. One more rider to go, then the winner would be announced. The next rider was fierce and competitive, but he didn't hold a candle to Westin. Of course, Silvia might be biased, but she turned out to be right.

When the announcer called out the name of Westin Farr as the winner, Silvia cheered.

"You're pretty excited about that bull rider," the woman next to her commented.

"He's my, uh, date tonight." She'd almost said "boyfriend," but that wouldn't be exactly true. Would it?

"Well, I'll be," the woman continued, patting her starched hairdo. "You've got yourself a catch, hon."

"Do you know him?"

"No, hon," she said. "But I have a good sense for things. Always have."

Silvia only smiled. They'd spent more time at "boulder stream," and Silvia had enjoyed every minute of it. In fact, the drive to the arena was nice, too. Westin had told her she needed to sit in the middle of the front bench, right next to him. "It's how cowboys and their ladies do it."

Silvia thought it was a bit cheesy, but she obliged, and she had no complaints about how Westin held her hand most of the drive. He hadn't kissed her since the stream—maybe he wasn't really into PDA, which only intrigued Silvia more.

What would it be like to date a cowboy? Well, she was getting ahead of herself. Sharing a few kisses at the stream earlier today had only established that she and Westin had chemistry between them. She already knew that, and it wouldn't be enough if things were to progress.

Not that she'd allow herself to think too far into the future. It was one of the topics discussed in group therapy. Keep it simple. Don't complicate what didn't need to be complicated. Which was exactly what she was doing on the ride back to the ranch today. She was creating scenarios that hadn't happened yet, as if she had the power to predict and control the future. And that only led her to panic.

But Westin hadn't been annoyed or angry or bothered. He'd pulled over to the side of the country road, and taken her on a walk, as if he knew exactly what she needed. And that kiss . . . Oh, boy. She was glad he'd repeated it, and she wouldn't mind a few other repeats.

The rodeo was nearly over, and the announcer was thanking the sponsors of the events.

"I think someone's looking for you, hon," the woman next to Silvia said.

Silvia looked to where the woman had nodded, and there he was. Walking toward their section, coming from the bucking chutes.

He was definitely searching for someone. Westin had changed out his helmet for his old cowboy hat. Silvia found herself smiling, and she stood and waved. At that moment, Westin saw her. The smile that broke out on his face went straight to her heart. She moved down the row, and by the time she got to the aisle, he was halfway up it.

A couple of people tried to get his attention to congratulate him, but he was solely focused on Silvia.

Her heart felt like it had leapt into her throat, and she found herself grinning as he closed the distance.

"How was that, darlin'?"

She laughed. "It was amazing, West, really." Was he just going to stand there, grinning? She threw her arms about his neck and hugged him. He flinched as if she'd hurt him, but then his arms came around her, and he held her close.

"You okay?" she asked, drawing back to look at him.

"Just a little sore."

"Oh, I'm sorry."

But he didn't let her pull away. "I'm glad you approve of my ride," he said, his voice a low rumble against her ear.

The crowd cheered as the announcer began to congratulate winners of the night's events, and still Silvia didn't let go, and neither did Westin.

Her heart was racing, and she could feel the rapid beat of his against her. Although his might be from bull riding, she was taking the chance that this man liked her as much as she liked him.

His hands moved slowly up her back, creating a trail of goosebumps.

"Are you sure you're okay?" she asked.

"I'm sure. And we can leave if you want," he said. "We don't have to stay."

She drew back to meet his gaze. "But don't you get recognized for winning your event?"

He shrugged a shoulder, his hands slipping to her waist. "It doesn't matter."

"Let's stay," she said. "You can sit with me. Come on." Bold of her, but Westin didn't seem to mind. She grasped his hand and led him back to her seat. There wasn't room, but they'd figure it out.

"Can you scoot over a little, sir?" Silvia asked in her sweetest tone.

The tobacco guy looked like he was about to grumble, but then his eyes widened at the sight of Westin.

"Congratulations, sir," the man said in a deep rasp. "I remember watching your father."

Westin extended his hand. "Thank you. It's good to hear people still remember him."

"Oh, he was unforgettable." The man released Westin's hand, then made room for him on the bench. "You're doing a fine job, son."

Westin nodded, and then he sat, keeping Silvia between the two of them.

"Oh, my," the woman on the other side said. "He really is your date."

Silvia smiled. "Westin, this is . . ."

"Lottie Barnes," the woman supplied. "Nice to meet you, young man. You've got yourself an enthusiastic fan here. I could hardly hear the announcer over her cheering."

Westin's green eyes fixed on her. "Is that so, darlin'?"

So what if she blushed? "Well, someone had to."

Westin chuckled, then he leaned close and kissed her cheek. "Thank you," he murmured in her ear.

So Silvia sat through the rest of the rodeo announcements, Westin at her side. He never let go of her hand, and she realized she could get quite used to this. Warm nights at the rodeo, a handsome cowboy by her side.

When the announcer congratulated Westin as the bull riding winner, he simply stood where he was and waved a thank you. The rodeo was over, and the crowds began to move into the aisles. They'd be clogged for a good while. Silvia was content to just sit and wait it out with Westin.

"You ever try the other events?" she asked as his thumb lazily traced circles on her wrist.

"Of course," he said, his thumb continuing its circles. "I've tried them all, from bareback to saddle bronc riding."

It was remarkable what a simple action from Westin could do to her heartrate.

"And . . . ?"

His mouth edged into a smile. "And I like bull riding better."

She nodded. Fair enough.

"What about team roping?"

"Tried it," he said, leaning close so she could hear over

the music that was blasting as the crowd continued exiting. "Still like bull riding better."

Silvia smiled.

"Well, let's go get my belt buckle. I left it with one of the officials. Then we'll get out of here," he said. "Sound good?"

"Yep."

He stood, keeping her hand in his, and pulling her to her feet. And that's how they walked through the arena, hand in hand. A small crowd seemed to be waiting for him once he collected his winning belt buckle.

Westin was surrounded by adults and kids alike, signing t-shirts and even a couple of cowboy hats. Silvia hovered in the background, waiting. A couple of young women, who looked like they'd put on three layers of makeup, approached Westin. They were maybe a few years younger than Silvia. It was clear what their aim was as they flirted and laughed.

"My friend was wondering if you have a girlfriend," the blonde with a white cowboy hat said.

"Or a wife," the redhead said with a giggle.

"I'm not married," Westin said, his tone friendly. "But I do have a special someone." When his gaze connected with hers across the space, Silvia knew she was blushing.

"Now, if you'll excuse me, ladies, I've kept my lady waiting long enough."

Silvia nearly gaped as he stepped around the women and headed toward her.

She set her hands on her hips as he neared and said, "Congratulations, Mr. Farr. Do you have a girlfriend or wife?"

He winked and draped an arm across her shoulders. "Let's get out of here, darlin'."

She smirked, but she also felt about ten feet tall walking out of the arena with him. Others stopped to congratulate him, but he only said, "Thank you, kindly," and continued walking.

Once they reached the truck, Westin opened the driver's door for her to get in on his side.

"Did you already bring out your gear?" she asked.

"Yeah, it's in the back," he said, handing her into the truck.

Not that she really needed help, but she appreciated his gentlemanly ways.

When he swung up next to her, she saw someone approaching his truck, waving.

"Who's that?" Silvia asked.

Westin turned his head, then rolled down his window.

The man was portly, his waist nearly as round as his height.

"Nice ride, West," he said. His thick mustache moved as he talked. "You're moving up, real quick."

"Thank you, Mr. Palmer," Westin said. "I appreciate you coming out."

"Wouldn't miss watching Bud Farr's son ride," Mr. Palmer continued. "Besides, this is my town. Named after my grandaddy."

Westin chuckled. "So it is." He reached out of the open window and shook the man's hand. "Nice to see you again."

"Take care of yourself, son." Mr. Palmer's gaze flitted toward Silvia, then locked onto her. His eyes narrowed, as if he were trying to see better into the cab of the truck. "And your lady there?"

"This is Silvia," Westin said immediately.

The man moved closer and rested his forearms on the window edge. His gaze was penetrating, and Silvia felt the back of her neck heat. Who was this guy, and why was he staring at her so hard?

"You from around here, miss?" Mr. Palmer said—his tone had a bit of an edge now.

The question sounded like a challenge. What did it matter where she was from? "No, Seattle, actually."

Mr. Palmer whistled. "You came a long way, little lady. Your folks speak English?"

She opened her mouth to reply, but no words came. Had he just said . . . ?

Mr. Palmer looked at Westin. "Can't find yourself a date in Texas?" he said with a chuckle. But it wasn't a friendly chuckle, it was more . . . in disgust.

Westin didn't answer the man's question directly. Instead, he said in a tight tone, "Do I need to step out of the truck, Mr. Palmer?"

The man raised his hands. "Ho now, we go way back, my friend."

Westin's jaw worked. "Then I suggest we say good night." He started up the truck, giving Mr. Palmer more than enough hint that Westin was serious about leaving.

Once Mr. Palmer backed away from the truck, Westin stepped on the gas and drove out of the parking lot. He'd left the window unrolled, and after a couple of minutes, the wind was starting to chill Silvia. When she shivered, Westin seemed to snap out of whatever his thoughts were, and he rolled up the window.

"Sorry about that," he murmured, then reached for her hand.

It was remarkable how just holding his hand eased the tension coiled inside of her. "Who was that guy?"

Westin sighed. "Palmer is one of those men who thinks he knows everything. Somehow, my dad was friends with him, although I could never understand why."

"So, he's just obnoxious?"

Westin glanced at her, then back to the road. "He's been known to protest against immigrants."

Silvia frowned.

"Against Mexicans, specifically."

"Oh." She really couldn't say anything else.

"I assume your grandparents are from somewhere in South America," Westin added, "but it doesn't really matter to me."

"My *parents* are from Mexico," Silvia said in a quiet tone. "My mom has citizenship in America, although I'm not sure about my dad. I never asked."

Westin tightened his hold on her hand as they slowed at the next traffic light. "Palmer is not representative of Texas. We just had the misfortune of running into him tonight."

Silvia didn't speak for a moment. In Seattle, she was known as Axel Diaz's sister, and no one messed with their family. In Lost Creek, she'd never been looked at sideways or talked down to. But this was a conversation they needed to have anyway. "Have you ever dated someone who's not Caucasian, Westin?"

He didn't answer for a moment, then he said, "No."

She drew her hand away. "Look, I've dated different guys, but I know some families are really traditional. You know, 'date your own kind' type of thing. And if that's your family, Westin, then I'm sorry, but I'm not going to get in the middle of any of that. I don't even want this to be an issue. Besides, my brother has the habit of hijacking all of my relationships with men. He's even gone so far as to show up on a doorstep and make threats. So it's probably better that we—"

"Stop," Westin said, cutting her off.

He slowed the truck, then pulled over to the side of the road. They were near a gas station, and the fluorescent lights filtered in through the front window.

He turned toward her, and she met his gaze.

"Look, your brother is not the one I want to date. He

doesn't scare me. And all I know is that it took a lot to drive away from Palmer. What I really wanted to do was punch the taste out of his mouth," he said. "I don't want to be around guys like him or people who are close-minded and hard-hearted."

He was staring at her with an intensity that she suspected he used only when bull riding.

"Silvia," he said in a softer voice. "You're beautiful. You're sweet. You're talented. Every minute I spend with you makes me happy. And I love that you have no problem setting me in my place." He draped his arm across the seat behind her, bringing them closer together. "My family will love you, if they ever meet you, if things between us . . . continue."

"Do you want us to continue?" she whispered, because her throat was too tight to speak normally.

He rested his other hand on her shoulder, his thumb brushing her collarbone. "Definitely."

She released a sigh. She could smell his soap, mixed with perspiration and dirt from the rodeo. She didn't mind. It only made him more authentically cowboy. "Okay, then let's forget about Mr. Palmer."

"My plan exactly." His gaze scanned her face, then he moved closer, and pressed his mouth against her jawline. His stubble had started to grow again, and his lips were warm against her cool skin. "What do *you* want, darlin'?" he whispered when he drew back a couple of inches. "Are we going to continue?"

As if she could think straight when he was touching her like this.

He leaned close again and pressed his mouth against the edge of her lips.

Here she was, sitting in an old truck with a bull rider, outside a small Texas gas station, and it was perhaps the most romantic moment she'd ever experienced.

She turned her face a fraction of an inch and pressed her mouth against his. The kiss was slow, sweet, and it sent her pulse in a hundred different directions. She slid her arms around his neck, and his hands moved over her back, then he pulled her even closer.

"Is that a yes?" he murmured against her mouth.

"Mm-hmm," she murmured back.

He chuckled, then kissed her harder, deeper, more fiercely.

Silvia clung to him as she met his every touch with her own, and her worried thoughts of the future seemed to slip away. She wondered if she'd ever had a more perfect end to a long day.

CHAPTER 18

BEFORE CLIMBING OUT OF his truck and checking into the next small-town rodeo event, a text came in. Westin opened the message from Axel Diaz.

How are you doing, man? Any updates on Silv that you can share with me? I've talked to her once, and she gave me homework. LOL. Which I'm doing, but she told me not to call until I was finished. Just looking for anything I should know.

A handful of days ago, Westin would have replied immediately, giving the guy whatever updates on his sister he asked for.

But now . . . things had changed with Silvia. After the night they ran into Mr. Palmer, Westin had felt more protective of her. Not only around strangers who were bullheaded, but because he knew she wanted to set boundaries with her brother.

Westin would be crossing those boundaries if he continued this texting strand with her brother. Westin was pretty sure Silvia wouldn't be too happy about it, which meant he had to tell her.

And that thought made his stomach knot up.

He'd seen her temper, he very well knew her stubbornness, and he also knew she was vulnerable right now. She'd shared personal things with him, about her brother, about some of the guys she'd dated—who were thankfully in the past—about her mom, about how she didn't remember her dad who had abandoned the family... Westin also knew her insecurities and fears about supplying barbeque sauce to Mariah's and what would happen if it took off and sold well.

Westin wished he was in Lost Creek right now so he could talk to Silvia in person. Telling her over the phone about her brother's texts wouldn't be such a great idea. He exhaled and closed his eyes. What to do? How to handle this?

If he told Axel the truth, it would go something like this: *I spent two days with her last week, and she's amazing and talented and sometimes lost and confused, but that's changing, and she's discovering her passions in life and what she really wants to accomplish. Oh, and I think I'm falling in love with her.*

He could only imagine Axel's reaction.

Westin was no stranger to black eyes, but he also didn't want to be a division between two siblings.

Another text came through. From Silvia.

Good luck tonight, West. Did I tell you that you're my favorite cowboy?

Yep. He was falling in love with her. He had about thirty minutes before he had to check in for the bull riding event in this town. This one was about a five-hour drive from Lost Creek, so he hadn't been able to work in seeing Silvia since last weekend.

Thanks, darlin'. Did I tell you that you're my favorite everything?

Haha. You're a sap.

I won't deny it. And good luck with your meeting tonight.

I think I'm going to lock myself in my bedroom.

Don't you dare.

Kidding. Sort of.

You'll be fine. Just listen to your gut. You'll know how to manage things.

Silvia's barbeque sauce had been a success at Mariah's Bakery this past week, attracting attention from surrounding towns. A grocery store distributor had talked to Mariah, who'd directed them to Silvia. And tonight, the distributor was going to meet with Silvia and talk about a possible contract.

It was all going so fast, but Westin was proud of her. She refused to let her brother know, and Westin didn't have the best knowledge of this type of business, but one of the women at the ranch had once owned a mom-and-pop shop. Glory someone. She'd be in the meeting, too.

Silvia's text chimed. *I wish I had as much confidence in myself as you seem to have in me.*

Westin really wanted to call her, to hear her voice, to tell her just how amazing she truly was. But he also knew their next phone call needed to be about his communication with Axel. How could he skirt around that when he was talking to her? As much as he wanted the weight of his upcoming confession off his chest, it would have to wait until he wasn't about to go ride in an event, and she was about to attend a major meeting.

Then just borrow my belief in you tonight, darlin', he wrote. *I'll call you when I'm done with my event and see how it went.*

She merely marked his text with a thumbs-up, so he took that as she was now focusing on her meeting. Which was good.

He climbed out of his truck and gathered up his gear, then he headed into the arena. Tonight wasn't a big competition night, not as far as the other bull riders who'd entered the event. But he also couldn't let his guard down. He thought of how Silvia was doing something hard tonight, and so he could do something hard as well. Stay focused, ride well, and not get injured.

Well, that last bit might be hard to control, because his shoulder had never really recovered from being thrown that day in Lost Creek a few weeks ago. Yeah, he was able to manage the pain with some ibuprofen, but he couldn't really baby it during competitions. His only solution was to skip a few workouts here and there, so he didn't aggravate it.

Besides, it would heal. Eventually. It had to. He knew he should get it looked at by a doctor, but frankly, Westin didn't want to hear bad news. Surgery for a bull rider usually meant his career was over. And he wasn't ready for that to happen.

"West, I didn't know you were coming."

Westin turned at the sound of the familiar voice. Lars was standing with a few other cowboys, none of whom he recognized.

West walked over to greet everyone, and Lars introduced them to each other.

"Oh, so you're Bud Farr's kid?" said one of the younger cowboys, who'd been introduced as Mike. "That guy could ride."

Westin smiled. He heard this a lot, and it was true, so he never contradicted it. But he could hold his own as well.

Lars clapped him on the back. "Well, you boys are in for a real treat tonight. Westin here is even better."

"Hold up, man," Westin said. "I wouldn't go that far."

"I'm up for a bet," Mike cut in.

The other guys laughed, and before Westin could say one more thing, they were all placing bets on his ride.

With a laugh, Westin said, "You guys can do what you want. I'm not having any part of this. Good luck to y'all." He tipped his hat and headed toward the bullpens to check out the livestock.

Lars caught up with him. "Hey, man, how's it going?"

"Good." Westin looked over at him. "You riding saddle bronc?"

"Yep."

Westin never knew with Lars, since the guy could do several events. Westin had tried them all, but like his dad, he kept coming back to bull riding.

They reached the livestock pen, and Westin draped his arms over the fence to watch the bulls. He'd find out who he drew soon enough, but for now, he wanted to check all of them out.

Lars joined him at the fence, leaning against it as well. "You ride any of these before?"

"That tan one," Westin said, pointing to one about a dozen feet away. "Name's Brutus."

Lars chuckled. "Sounds about right." Then he looked over at Westin. "Hey, if you ever need to talk, let me know."

Westin frowned. "What are you talking about?"

Lars shrugged. "Just have a feeling, bro, that you're struggling with something. Is it being faced with memories of your dad at all these rodeos? I know he's been gone for a while, but it can still be tough. Not that I'm an expert—I mean, I barely knew *my* dad."

Lars had been raised by his grandparents. He'd been one of those kids who'd sort of floated through life. Was up for anything. Never really had roots. Which meant he could spend as much time or as little time as he wanted in one place. Rodeo gave him enough of a paycheck to live day to day, and he also took up odd jobs in maintenance or construction to fill in the rest.

Lars's usually warm hazel eyes were assessing Westin as if he were trying to figure out something.

"Well, it's not what you think, if you're asking," Westin said.

Lars's gaze remained steady. "I'm asking."

Westin blew out a breath, then he took off his cowboy hat and scrubbed his fingers through his hair. Replacing his hat, he said, "Okay, might as well get the load off."

Lars just nodded, keeping his gaze on the livestock.

It was one thing that Westin liked about Lars. He voiced his opinion—and it could be strong—but he also knew when it was time to listen.

"Here's the thing," he said. "The guys have razzed me about Silvia Diaz, and, well . . ."

"I won't say anything, if that's what you're asking."

Westin gave a short nod. "Thanks. She's amazing, Lars. And I think we might have a future, but there are a lot of complications. Barriers, maybe."

Lars said nothing, but he was listening.

So Westin gave him the basics of Silvia wanting to have a better relationship with her brother, but also be more independent. But now, Westin was stuck in the middle. Reporting to Axel, and trying to figure things out with Silvia at the same time.

After Westin finished with what he was willing to share, with what he felt didn't infringe too much on Silvia's privacy, he said, "I know I need to talk to Silvia first. But what about Axel? How do I handle him?"

"Silvia's your priority," Lars said immediately. "The relationship is between you. Not her brother, not any of us."

Westin nodded. This was true. "I'm worried she's going to bail on me after finding out that I've been talking to her brother behind her back."

Lars drew in a breath. "Better now than down the road, when you have your heart involved."

"Too late for that."

Lars clapped a hand on Westin's shoulder. Thankfully, it was his good one. "It's still the right thing to do."

"Yeah, I know." Westin rubbed a hand over his face. "I'm going to tell her after the rodeo tonight. I wanted to talk to her in person, but the phone will have to do."

Despite the talk with Lars, and Westin's determination to talk to Silvia after the rodeo, his stomach remained in knots. There wasn't another option right now. She was in her meeting, and he had no idea how long that would last.

Whoever bet on Westin's win that night won, and won big. He outrode everyone else in the bull riding, and walked away with a tidy purse. Lars and the others congratulated him, then invited him to join them at a local grub house.

Westin turned them down, intent on having a conversation with Silvia. And if it didn't go well, he probably wouldn't want to be social.

When he called Silvia, it went straight to voicemail.

Did she have her phone off?

He sent a text instead. *How'd it go? Call me when you can.*

And then he watched the clock as he drove to a drive-thru and grabbed a chicken sandwich and a drink. Still, she didn't text back. He finished his meal, and another thirty minutes passed. Nothing from Silvia.

He checked the time again, and wondered if she was in some sort of activity, but it was nearly eleven p.m. She'd told him that they had their own time after nine p.m. So, where was she? Maybe chatting with Kellie? Maybe the meeting with the distributor had gone well, and they were putting together some sort of business plan?

Or maybe she was sitting on the porch in the nice summer night.

She could even be asleep.

He pulled up his texts, trying to distract himself from his circling thoughts. The Chute was in full force, and Lars had been true to his word—nothing about Silvia.

Lars: *Shoutout to West. Another win tonight. Can't stop him.*

Ford: *Nice job, W.*

Ryan: *You're the man, as always.*

Eric: *Can I interview you yet, West? Pretty soon, you'll be too big for us small potatoes.*

Ford: *I agree—we need screen time for West.*

Eric: *Just name the time and place. I'll come to you. West, you there?*

Ford: *Too busy with his lady?*

Reid: *What did I miss? W, you getting serious?*

It was time for Westin to intervene. *Thanks, guys. I already told you, Silvia is none of your business. And, Eric, that's a no. Maybe when I reach my dad's score.*

Eric: *Oh, come on, man. You've got your own name.*

Reid: *Why you keeping Silvia to yourself? Ryan has spilled his guts out to anyone who will listen.*

Ford posted a GIF with a blubbering dude.

Ryan added one with an eye roll.

Eric texted: *Back on topic. West, I want you on my channel. You can talk about whatever you want. No pressure.*

Westin shook his head. Eric wouldn't give up. Maybe it would happen, maybe not.

His phone started to ring. Westin's pulse leapt. Was Silvia calling? But the Caller ID said Axel.

Was this just a check-in, or had something happened to Silvia? Was that why she hadn't answered his texts?

"What's up?" Westin said, hoping that his panic didn't sound in his voice.

"Of all the phone calls I've made this week, this is the last thing I thought I'd have to deal with." Axel's voice came through rough. Upset.

"Is Silvia okay?" Westin asked, not caring what his own voice sounded like right now. Why else would her brother be calling so late at night?

"You tell me, cowboy," Axel ground out. "It seems that you've been dating my sister, while she's at a freaking recovery center. That's the lowest, dirtiest—"

"Hold up," Westin cut in. Obviously, Axel had found out—from Silvia? Kellie? Someone else? But what exactly had been said didn't matter right now. "Silvia is an adult. You might be her brother, but she can make her own decisions about who she dates. And believe me, none of this was planned." New thoughts entered Westin's mind. What if Silvia complained about him to her brother? What if she didn't like him as much as he liked her? Maybe this was how she got rid of guys—she'd told him more than one story about her brother confronting the guys she dated.

Was this how it worked in their family?

Westin's thoughts jumbled. He couldn't make assumptions about Silvia right now, or he'd go crazy.

"Planned or not, that's no excuse," Axel bit out. "I trusted you, man. You were supposed to watch out for her and report back to me."

"Exactly," Westin said. "And that's what I did. The rest is . . . between her and me."

"Like hell it is."

Westin closed his eyes and tried to even out his breathing. It didn't help that Silvia was ignoring his calls and Lost Creek was five hours away. "Look, I don't know what she said to you, but if you're asking me, I'm all in."

Axel's chuckle was low... but not friendly at all. "You've got a lot of nerve, I'll give you that. Stay away from my sister, Westin Farr. That's your only warning."

Westin leaned forward, gripping the steering wheel of his truck with one hand. "Why? So you can call the shots for the rest of her life? So you can stifle her dreams? Control her every move? Keep her in your big, fat, pro-baseball shadow?"

"Stay out of my relationship with my sister," Axel spat out.

Westin knew he'd hit a nerve, but it gave him no satisfaction.

Axel wasn't finished. "My sister is off-limits—"

"If Silvia wants to call things off, she'll tell me herself," Westin cut in. "Now, I'd appreciate it if you'd stay in your own lane, Mr. Diaz."

"You throwing therapy jargon at me?"

"Damn right, I am."

When Westin hung up with Axel Diaz, he wanted to erase the entire night. Go back to before the rodeo. Call Silvia like a man and tell her what had transpired between him and Axel. Apologize. Beg for her forgiveness.

Now there was only one thing to do. Find her and do it in person.

He started the truck and headed out of town. If he started driving now, he'd be in Lost Creek by dawn.

CHAPTER 19

SILVIA HADN'T SLEPT MUCH. How could she? After ignoring the calls and texts from Westin, she'd finally turned off her phone and gone to bed. To stare at the ceiling.

Her brother had called a few minutes after her meeting to tell her he'd finished the reading material, and she was on such a high from all the good news from the distributor that she spilled the beans. And then she'd mentioned Westin.

"Wait, what?" Axel had said. "Westin has been helping you? What do you mean?"

Silvia's heart sank. She should have left Westin out of the entire conversation, but it was too late. She tried to keep what she told Axel very platonic, but it was like he could see right through her casual remarks.

She should have stood up to him, should have defended her and Westin's relationship. Instead, she'd cowered and become the seventeen-year-old again who let her brother make decisions for her.

Her mind was racing so fast, and her heart beating so hard, that she hadn't used any of the communication skills she'd learned over the past two weeks. She hadn't told Axel that he didn't get a say in who she dated anymore.

Flashes of memories returned throughout the night. Guys she'd dated, guys she knew weren't right for her, guys who Axel told her to break up with—or he would take care of it. Which had happened a time or two. When she'd finally moved to college, it meant freedom to date who and when she wanted. But Axel always found out eventually.

And then he dropped the bomb.

And it had silenced her. Stunned her.

Apparently, Axel was talking to Westin on the side. Behind her back. Checking in about her. Even though Silvia thought she was finally getting a handle on her life and becoming independent by putting up boundaries with her brother, Axel had found a way around them. And Westin was part of it.

The guy she was liking more each day, the guy who she was starting to see a future with, had betrayed her.

It was then that Silvia had hung up on her brother. She couldn't hear one more word from him that night. Her mind was a tangled mess, and her heart was even worse.

As the sun rose in the morning, Silvia wasn't sure she'd slept at all. She'd gone through every emotion known to humankind. Anger, regret, sorrow, disappointment, and now, she was just plain mad. At her brother, but even more so at Westin. She knew her brother, expected him to be what he was, but Westin?

She'd started to believe. She'd let down her guard with him. She'd told him so much about her family—things she'd never told anyone. Take away the intimacies they'd shared, and what really hurt was that she felt like she'd lost a friend, when she'd never had many of those.

Silvia climbed out of bed and changed into her running

clothes. Even though she was physically exhausted from so little sleep, she needed to get out in the fresh air. Clear her head. Because the one idea that kept coming back to her would be the most daring thing she'd ever done in her life.

She headed into the kitchen and got a glass of water, making sure not to make any noise that might wake someone in the house. At least a couple of the women had heard her tearful conversation with her brother. Glory had knocked on the door after it, but Silvia had said she didn't want to talk about it to anyone.

If anyone happened into the kitchen right now, they'd be scared off by Silvia's puffy eyes and pale face. As she walked to the front door, she wrapped her hair into a ponytail. She hadn't bothered to brush it—besides, there was no one to see when you lived on a ranch in the middle of nowhere.

She did a couple of stretches on the front porch as she breathed in the clean, cool morning air. The temperature was perfect, and by the time she returned to the ranch house, she knew it would be plenty warm. She began a slow jog down the driveway. Today, she'd stay on the road, not cut across any fields. Her exhaustion might lead her to not pay attention and step in a hole or something. And the last thing she needed was a twisted ankle.

She had a long day ahead of her if all went according to plan.

And those plans . . . she was done, with everything. Kellie, the women's ranch, Axel, Westin, and all those rodeo guys.

She would talk to Mariah about finding a room to rent in town. She had enough money from the sale of her barbeque sauce to pay for a cheap room. All she needed was one room to sleep in and keep her things. Then she'd look for a space to begin her business.

The distributor had given her a contract last night that

she'd signed. He said he'd pay for rent in a location of her choosing where she could set up shop to make the barbeque sauce, and he would pay for the equipment and supplies. Last night, it seemed to be all happening too fast, but this morning, it couldn't happen fast enough.

As Silvia left the main driveway of the ranch and jogged along the bend that would eventually connect to the road that headed into town, she slowed to a stop.

There was a red truck parked off to the side of the road.

She was well familiar with that truck, and she knew instantly it couldn't belong to anyone else but Westin Farr.

But what was it doing here? She was pretty sure he'd driven his truck to the rodeo. Could he have taken something else? But as she began to move again, she could see that someone was in the driver's seat.

Her heart pounded in disbelief as she drew closer. Westin was here. Asleep in his truck. He must have driven all night after she refused to pick up her phone.

She continued past, hoping he wouldn't wake up. But if he did, then she'd tell him exactly how she felt about his betrayal. If he didn't, then she could run in peace.

Westin didn't move, and she couldn't see most of his face since he'd pulled his hat forward. Probably to block out the moon that no longer shone above.

She started to jog again, and with every step, she was determined to cut all men out of her life for a while. Weeks, maybe months. Including her brother.

He might put up a fuss, but she'd stand strong. She had to do this, on her own.

"Silvia."

No, it wasn't Westin's voice. She was just imagining it.

"Silvia, wait up," Westin called after her.

She continued jogging and didn't look back. She might

have even picked up her pace a little. When she heard the thud of his footsteps—cowboy boots, to be more exact—she looked over.

Yep, he was jogging with her, keeping up, a couple of steps behind. In his boots and jeans and button-down shirt. At least he wasn't wearing his cowboy hat. That would have been ridiculous.

She couldn't help but notice the lines about his eyes. He was tired, too. Good, he should be.

She looked forward again. Maybe he'd tire out, or his feet would start to hurt. She kept jogging, nearing the main road now. And Westin continued to run beside her.

Neither of them spoke. Silvia wasn't about to speak first, and she wasn't going to answer him if he said anything to her.

Still, they ran.

The morning chill had faded, and heat prickled through her, although she was sure it was because of the man running with her, and not due to the rising sun. The landscape stretched out in fields of green, dotted with groups of trees. It was quiet, beautiful, and should be more peaceful. This run was about collecting her thoughts and solidifying her decisions.

In her mind, Westin was already in the past.

And her legs were starting to burn. How long had she been running? She was well down the main road leading into town. Maybe she should just head all the way into town. See what Westin did then. But she didn't want to be trapped there, because she doubted she could muster the energy to run back.

Westin's breathing was as heavy as hers now, and he must be sweating up a storm, too.

Yeah, he was a bull rider, but that was a different set of muscles than straight running for miles.

Time to turn around.

She did an about face and began running the opposite direction.

Westin changed directions, too. Dang it.

Even if she did want to talk, she was too out of breath to yell at him like he deserved.

Their footsteps pounded in sync, and when a truck passed them on the road, Silvia became hyper aware of how ridiculous they must look running together. She in her jogging clothes, him in his jeans and boots.

At the next shady spot, she slowed down, then stopped and began to stretch.

Westin stopped, too, of course. This, she expected. He didn't stretch, though. Instead, he folded his arms and watched her.

When she'd stretched everything she could think of, twice, she finally looked at him.

And dang, he was still handsome in his rugged way, with those murky green eyes of his and that scar along his jaw. His shirt collar was open, and she could see the perspiration on his chest as it rose and fell from still catching his breath.

Well, she was still out of breath, too.

"Can we talk about this?" Westin asked, his voice low, his gaze searing into her.

"About how you went behind my back and reported to my *brother*?"

His gaze fell, and his jaw tightened. "Yeah. I can explain."

It was Silvia's turn to fold her arms. She shouldn't even allow him an explanation, but she was still a mile from the ranch, and she might as well get it over with. "Go ahead."

Westin seemed surprised. His gaze lifted, and he rubbed the back of his neck. "Axel reached out to me the day after I met you and you were already at the ranch. We'd made that dinner, and then you came to the rodeo. It was before I knew all of your issues with him. I told him you were doing fine, that's about it."

Silvia kept her arms folded. They both knew there was more to this than just a few texts.

Westin set his hands on his hips. "Look, it was harmless. I swear. And when he kept texting me, and then you and I were getting . . . closer, I started to think maybe it wasn't a good idea anymore."

"You think?"

Westin sighed. "I was going to tell you, was planning on telling you—"

"But let me guess," Silvia cut in. "You were flattered that a pro-baseball player was your buddy. You were giving him what he wanted, and that made you feel good about yourself." Her eyes burned hot, and she hated that she was on the verge of crying in front of Westin. "Never mind what *I* might think or feel. It's the same with all men. You put yourselves first, always. Your pride, your ego, it's all about *you*—" She turned then, because the tears were coming, and she had to be by herself. Not looking at a guy who'd broken her heart.

"Hold up, darlin'," Westin said, grasping her arm before she could leave.

"Don't call me that," she said. "Not anymore."

He dropped his hand. "My apologies . . . Silvia, I messed up, I know that. And I'm sorry. But I'm also not finished explaining."

She wiped at her eyes and took a shaky breath. "Continue."

"When I was in Oklahoma, I could feel that things were changing with us," he said. "At least with me. I didn't know what to expect, but our texts and calls gave me hope where I hadn't allowed myself to consider anything between us."

Silvia looked away. She'd felt the same, but she had also

wondered about his ex-girlfriend. He still hadn't said anything about her. She snapped her gaze back to him. "What happened between you and Amy while you were there? You never told me."

Westin's brow furrowed. "Nothing happened between us. I told her she needed help with her addictions, and I even put together an intervention. Didn't go so well, but I had to try." He shrugged. "Only time will tell if she'll get cleaned up one day, but it's out of my hands."

Silvia stared. Of all the things she expected him to say about his ex-girlfriend, this wasn't it. "She's an addict?"

"Yeah," Westin said. "In denial about it, though. I talked to Kellie about how to help her, and she gave me some good leads. She also said I had to step away if I wasn't going to pursue a relationship with Amy, or else she'd become dependent on me as one of her supports. And since I already knew my heart was elsewhere, it wasn't a hard decision to make. I wish Amy all the best, of course. I hope she'll find her way back to a good life someday."

Silvia's tears had dried, and she felt the niggling of warmth spread to her chest. Westin was a good man. Even she could recognize that despite his betrayal of her. She took a step back, because being this close to Westin was making her change her mind about him.

"I should have told you about Amy," Westin said. "I didn't realize you'd been wondering about that."

Silvia shrugged. "Doesn't matter now, does it?"

He didn't respond to that. Instead, he said, "Yesterday, Axel texted me about you right before I got to the arena. I didn't answer because I knew I had to talk to you first. I can show you on my phone if you want."

Silvia shook her head.

"I was torn up," he said. "I knew you would be upset, but

it was still my only course of action. You were so excited about the meeting with the distributor that I decided to tell you later in the night, after the rodeo and after your meeting."

She could believe him, but what did it matter? There was all the time between last night and when they'd kissed, and he was still talking to Axel behind her back—that was what bothered her. If she was ever going to be an independent adult, the man she dated couldn't be controlled by her brother. "What bothers me most, Westin, is that after I confided in you about my issues with my brother, and told you about my dad and my mom, you *still* went behind my back. And... then we kissed, and I know I've dated a lot, and you've dated, too, but I thought it meant..." She broke off. "Never mind. It doesn't matter now, does it? You obviously considered me a fling, and you've made your loyalty clear. If I ever date a man seriously, then it's going to be one who can stand on his own two feet."

She took another step back. Westin was staring at her like she'd slapped him. And she was glad. Who cared if she'd been harsh? It was needed. She'd said her piece. She'd spoken her mind. And as far as she was concerned, this was the last time she'd see Westin Farr.

She turned and started walking toward the ranch. This time, Westin didn't grasp her arm or try to stop her.

But he did say one last thing, and it almost made her turn around. Almost.

"Silvia, you were never a fling, and I hope you can forgive me for not telling you about Axel."

She continued to walk, but his voice carried through the quiet morning.

"I'll be waiting if you can ever forgive me."

She blinked back the second round of tears that had started. This wasn't about forgiveness. Sure, she could forgive him for not telling her, but how did she really know he was going to tell her last night? It would have been too late then, as well. He should have told her from the very first text. How could she trust a man who wasn't transparent?

Ironically, Axel was nothing but transparent.

She wiped at the tears on her cheeks and began to jog again. The sooner she was back at the ranch, the sooner she could pack up and get out of there. Yep, she'd decided—she was leaving the ranch today.

No footsteps followed. No cowboy caught up.

That was fine. Westin could sit on the side of the road for the rest of the day for all she cared.

She hated that she was crying over him. She'd spent enough time doing that—all night. And she hated the way her heart tugged when his red truck came into view. And she hated that he told her he'd be waiting for her.

Well, he'd be waiting for about a hundred years.

CHAPTER 20

"What do you mean, she's *gone*?" Westin asked Kellie.

He hadn't dared to go back to the women's ranch and knock on the door—although he'd been tempted. He'd waited for about half an hour after Silvia had jogged off. Then he'd walked back to his truck and headed over to Ryan's for a shower.

One look at Westin, and Ryan had demanded answers.

Westin told him the basics, much less than he'd told Lars, and Ryan had apparently talked to Kellie when Westin was in the shower.

So, here he and Kellie sat on Ryan's porch as Westin asked after Silvia. How she was doing was his primary concern. The bottom line was that he didn't want to put more stress in her life than what she was already dealing with.

But Kellie's frank declaration of Silvia leaving the ranch had rocked through him like an earthquake.

This was not good, not good at all.

Westin's careless mistake had just multiplied by a hundred.

"Packed up her stuff, and I took her into town," Kellie

said. "She's got a room to rent there, I guess, and she's going to give this barbeque sauce a valiant effort. She said I could tell people she's staying in Lost Creek, but nothing after that. So I've probably told you too much already."

Westin leaned forward and clasped his hands together. "Thanks for telling me." It was a huge relief that she was still in Lost Creek and hadn't disappeared into the unknown. And she hadn't taken off to Seattle, either. Good for her. She was going to have a successful business, he knew it. Her determination and stubbornness were the perfect combination, along with her talents.

He missed her.

Westin stood and began to pace the porch. "So, on a scale of one to ten, how mad do you think she is at me?"

Kellie groaned. "Do not go there, West. I'm staying out of this. I warned her against you—"

He stopped. "Wait, what? You warned *her* against *me*? Why?"

Kellie's blue eyes flashed. "It's not what you think. I warned her to not break your heart. From what Axel told me, she's had more than a few boyfriends."

"Whoa." Westin held up his hand. "Her past doesn't bother me. The past is the past. It applies to all of us."

"Point taken," Kellie said with a nod. "But you're my friend, West. You're like a brother, and Silvia is, well . . . one of those women who's either hot or cold. And I didn't want you to get hurt—which is what happened anyway."

Westin leaned against the porch railing and folded his arms. "It wasn't because she's hitting up other guys."

Kellie rose to her feet. "I know, but Silvia Diaz is a live wire. People aren't perfect, West, I get that. You aren't, she isn't, and heck, I'm far from it. But what happens when you screw up again?"

"Who says that I'll—"

"You're human," Kellie cut in. "Just think about it, West, before you get on your white horse and go charging after her with flowers and sweet words. Maybe she's not the right woman for you—once those rose-colored glasses of yours come off."

Westin straightened. "I'm twenty-eight, Kell. I'm not a kid anymore, and I think I know my own mind."

"Just saying." Kellie moved past him to the top of the stairs. "I've warned you. And now I'm staying out of it."

Westin exhaled. "Thanks for letting me know where she went. And don't worry, I'm not going to charge after her, especially on a white horse. She doesn't even like horses."

Kellie's mouth twitched as if she were holding back a laugh. "Well, good luck with whatever you decide to do. But my advice is to stick to your rodeo circuit and wait for another woman to come along. One a little less . . . impassioned."

Westin rubbed the back of his neck. He'd known Kellie for years, and she knew her stuff in the therapy world, but this advice just didn't sit right. "Thanks again, Kell."

She nodded, then headed down the porch steps. He remained on the porch until she climbed into her truck and drove away.

Then he went into the house to find Ryan. Westin needed a distraction. Work. Something to keep him busy. Or he would be climbing in his truck and driving into town to make a fool out of himself. He'd already let Silvia know where he stood, and now the ball was in her court, so to speak.

Ryan was on the phone with someone talking about a lumber delivery that was apparently late. When he hung up, his blue eyes snapped to Westin. "Well, how did it go with Kellie?"

"Said that Silvia moved into town and is renting a room. Setting up a business to sell her barbeque sauce."

Ryan's brows shot up. "That's a real thing, then? I'm impressed."

Westin nodded.

"So . . . you're not leaving Lost Creek anytime soon, I take it?"

"If you don't mind, I'll stick around until I have to get to the next gig," Westin said. "That is, if you need any free labor around here, then I'm your man."

The smile on Ryan's face was slow. "Oh, you should not have said that. You're gonna regret every last word."

Westin chuckled. "Lay it on me. The harder the work, the better."

Ryan gave him a knowing nod. "Well, then. We're heading to the arena. We've got ourselves a new ticket booth to build. The lumber will be there within the hour."

"You're the contractor for it or something?"

"Something like that," Ryan said, scratching the several days growth of whiskers on his chin. "How I get roped into some things is beyond me. I got myself a life, unlike you."

Westin raised his brows. "How are things going with your lady?"

"Can't complain." Ryan flashed a quick grin. "Now let's get out of here. The sooner we start, the sooner I can see her."

Westin helped Ryan load the back of his truck with the tools they'd need, then they climbed into the cab. As they drove, Westin checked his phone and replied to a couple of things from The Chute. Things were quiet today since everyone was either traveling, working, or training.

An individual text from Lars read: *Hey, thinking about you, man. Hope things went well with Silvia.*

Westin wrote back: *She dumped me. Long story. Still in Lost Creek. I'll call when I break for lunch. Building some stuff with Ryan today.*

Lars's reply came immediately: *Wow. Sorry to hear that.*

Westin pocketed his phone and leaned his head back with a sigh.

Even though Ryan had the radio on, Westin couldn't focus on the song. He hated that he'd hurt Silvia. Kellie had it all wrong. Westin was the one who'd broken *her* heart, not the other way around. Well, his was pretty bruised, too.

He hadn't even told Silvia about the threats Axel had made to him. They didn't signify, anyway. Silvia had dumped him.

But she hadn't left Lost Creek.

Somehow, his aching heart was finding hope in that.

Because he was happy she was making this move and taking charge. Even if he couldn't be a part of her life, he wanted the best for her. The very best.

His phone chimed with a text, and he pulled it out. It was from Ellie, the woman from the rehab place in Oklahoma. His pulse skyrocketed as he opened the text. Would it be bad news or good news?

Amy checked into our facility last night. I thought you should know. I think she'll have a great future once she gets through this rough spot. Thanks for connecting us.

The relief that swept through Westin was two-fold. First, for Amy and her recovery. Second, that he didn't have to worry about his mom in the house alone anymore.

He forwarded the text to his sister Cheryl, and she replied with several celebrating emojis.

He hadn't told her about Silvia. He'd planned to hold off until things were more established between them, but now that was all a moot point.

"Hey, you coming?" Ryan asked.

Westin realized the truck had stopped and the radio was off. "Yeah."

Ryan was watching him, a question in his eyes, but Westin merely opened his door and climbed out. Then he started unloading tools from the bed of the truck.

It would be good to stay busy and work up a sweat. The morning had already heated up, and that was just fine with Westin. He'd forget that Silvia was somewhere down the road, not too far, if she was staying someplace in town.

Maybe they'd run into each other at some point. That was fine. They could be cordial. Westin's heart would heal. Eventually.

"Finally," Ryan muttered as he came around the truck, where Westin had picked up a saw.

Westin looked up to see a flatbed truck pulling into the rodeo parking lot. The lumber stacked on the bed of the truck looked freshly milled.

"I guess we're painting, too?"

"Yep," Ryan said with a chuckle. "We're doing the whole thing, from start to finish."

"How big are you thinking?"

Ryan looked toward the old ticket booth that Westin was glad would be torn down. There were gaping spaces between the slats, and the bottom looked as if it had been kicked in.

"Same size, I reckon," Ryan said. "A couple more guys are on their way. With your help, the work will go a lot faster. You're handy with a saw, right?"

"Yeah." Westin continued to unload the equipment as Ryan directed the flatbed truck driver how far to pull back.

Then everyone pitched in to unload the lumber. By that time, another truck had showed up, and two younger guys hopped out.

"West, this is Ben and Greg. They're calf ropers. Maybe you remember them?"

"Seen you around," Westin said, shaking each of their hands.

"Great to meet you," Ben said. He was the redhead, and he looked like he was a teenager, although he must be in his twenties.

"My dad was a big fan of your dad," Greg added, hooking his thumbs in his belt loops. "His perfect score is legendary. I think I've watched the video a hundred times."

Westin chuckled. "Yeah, he was right proud of that."

Ryan clapped a hand on Westin's shoulder, and he tried not to wince. "Westin here is set to match his daddy's record. Getting closer."

Westin chuckled, hiding his grimace. "Well, boys. That shed isn't gonna build itself."

They all set to work, following a blueprint Ryan had sketched out. Westin saw a couple of flaws in the plans, and Ryan made changes. All in all, the work went smoothly. Westin stayed quiet for the most part, listening to Ben and Greg's banter as they talked shop about other riders and rodeos.

Ryan paused plenty of times to text someone, and Westin bet it was his lady, but he wasn't going to give Ryan a hard time in front of the other guys.

If it was just the Original Six, then it would be an open field day.

Once all the boards were measured and cut, they began to nail them to the cross boards. The work was easy enough, but the sun was at full heat now. Ben and Greg stripped off their t-shirts, soon followed by Ryan taking off his button-down. They left their cowboy hats on, of course.

Heck, Westin was about to strip down to his birthday suit. Instead, he peeled off his shirt, which was ten shades of sweaty, then downed one of the water bottles from the back of the truck. It wasn't cold, but he was past caring.

"What happened to your shoulder, dude?" Greg asked.

Oops. Too late.

The bruising he'd gotten a few weeks ago at the Lost Creek arena had only intensified with the two subsequent rodeos. The pain ran deep now, and Westin had taken his fair share of ibuprofen. It wasn't something to be worried about, though—bruises were common—but he also hadn't wanted any attention about it. As long as he could still hang onto the bull riggin', he would still ride it out.

"Just a good workout at last night's rodeo," Westin said in a light voice. He picked up the nail gun again and set to work.

But Ryan strode over and took a closer look. "There's some old bruising here, and it's deep." He pressed two fingers against the back of Westin's shoulder, and it nearly made him jump out of his skin.

"Easy there," Ryan said. "You okay?"

What Westin wouldn't give for an ice pack right now. "Fine, man, just didn't expect you to get cozy on me."

Ryan didn't laugh.

In fact, both Ben and Greg were staring at him.

"I'm fine," Westin insisted. "Still works. Just looks ugly."

"You gonna get that looked at, West?" Ryan said in a low, even tone.

Westin took off his hat and swiped the perspiration from his forehead. He was even hotter when standing around. "I aim to."

"When?" Ryan asked, his blue eyes the color of steel.

"Soon."

"Before the next rodeo?"

"I'll see how it feels in a day or two." Westin moved past him and drilled into the boards. After a handful of seconds, everyone was back to work. The time flew, and for that, he was grateful. Surely, he'd sleep well tonight. He could forget about . . . everything . . . for a few hours, at least.

"I'm ordering lunch," Ryan said. "What do you want from Mariah's Café?"

At the mention of the café, of course, Westin's mind returned to thoughts of Silvia. "I'll have one of those chicken sandwiches."

"Oh, you gotta try the barbeque chicken plate she just added to the menu," Ben said. "I had it twice yesterday."

Greg chuckled. "No wonder you're putting on the pounds."

Ben scoffed and shoved Greg in the shoulder.

"Sure," Westin said with a shrug. "I'll get the barbeque chicken plate."

Ryan's gaze connected with Westin's, then he looked away. He knew exactly why there was a new menu item at the café.

"Great." Ryan turned away to make the call.

"You guys gonna help me?" Westin ground out as he lifted one side of the pre-made roof.

Ben and Greg hurried to pick up the other edges, and they lifted it together. Ryan jumped in, and with the roof on the newly-built shed, it was finally looking decent.

"You picked up the paint, right?" Ryan asked Ben.

"Sure did," he said. "Got that baby blue."

Ryan narrowed his eyes. "Tell me you're kidding."

Ben laughed. "Don't worry, boss. Got the pearly white."

Ryan set his hands on his hips.

"Kidding again." Ben was still chuckling as he headed to his truck. He came back with two gallons of rust red and a pint of black for trim work.

"How long until that food gets here?" Greg complained.

"Keep working, and it will be here soon enough," Ryan said, glancing over at West. "How you holding up with that shoulder?"

Westin scowled. "Fine, doc. If I want your advice, I'll ask for it."

"Ha." Ryan cracked open one of the paint cans. "That'll be the day."

CHAPTER 21

SILVIA HAD ALL KINDS of plans to fix up this room over the café. Mariah was renting it out to her for free if Silvia helped out in the café for a few hours a day. Of course, Silvia accepted. Free rent for a place to live? Even though the place needed fixing up, it was a steal. She'd still have plenty of time to make the barbeque sauces until . . . until it took off like the distributor thought it would.

He'd even said she needed to start thinking about hiring employees.

It was all so mindboggling, and new. She shouldn't get ahead of herself, either.

Silvia shut the door on the grungy space. Soon, she'd have it spic and span with curtains and stuff hanging on the wall. But for now, she'd pitch in at the café. Leaving the ranch had been harder than she'd expected. All the ladies had given her hugs and wished her all the best. Glory had insisted that Silvia keep the black hat and black boots.

"I'm done with rodeos," Silvia had declared.

Glory had simply smiled and set the hat and boots in her hands. "You're living in Texas now. Mandatory accessories."

Silvia had almost teared up, but the women promised they'd be coming into town to see her, and she could still join in any of their sessions or activities. She might. She hadn't decided yet. Right now, she needed some space.

The café was surprisingly busy, and it wasn't even noon. She jumped in to help take orders, although she bungled a few of them up.

"You'll get the hang of it soon enough, sweetie," Mariah said with a laugh when Silvia accidentally gave a customer a dozen cookies instead of a dozen cupcakes.

Remembering what everyone was saying seemed to be a skill Silvia lacked. Maybe it was part of why she struggled in school.

The phone rang, and Mariah was ringing up a customer, so she said, "Can you get that, Silvia?"

"Sure." She headed to the phone. "Mariah's Bakery & Café," she answered, mimicking what she'd heard previously.

The female caller said, "I'd like to order two of the full-sized chicken pot pies, and I'll be there in ten minutes to pick them up."

Even Silvia knew it took more than ten minutes to cook a pot pie. She looked over at Mariah, who was still busy.

Silvia swallowed, then said, "I'm sorry, but they take thirty minutes to bake. I can get them in the oven now if you'd like. What's your name?"

The woman's laugh was dry. "I don't want them cooked, dear. They're for dinner later tonight. I'll pick them up pre-made, but not *pre-cooked*."

Silvia closed her eyes. "Ah. That makes more sense."

The woman laughed again. "See you in ten." She hung up before Silvia could ask for her name again.

"You okay?" Mariah asked.

"You need to answer the next phone call," Silvia declared. "I'll help with anything else but that."

Mariah chuckled. "All right."

Silvia worked at the register, then cleaned tables—both easy tasks.

"We've got four barbeque chicken plates on order, but they have to be delivered," Mariah said to Silvia. "Do you mind doing the delivery?"

Silvia looked over at her in surprise. "We do deliveries?"

"Sometimes," Mariah said, her eyes twinkling. "Depends on who it is."

"Ooh, is there something I should know?" Silvia teased.

"Oh, nothing like that," Mariah said with a laugh. "One is my brother. Now, off with you. They're at the rodeo arena, building a new ticket booth, I guess. Take my SUV."

"Will do," Silvia said and set the covered barbeque chicken plates into a box Mariah pointed out. Then she added four large drinks, and with Mariah's permission, she slipped in a sack of fresh cookies.

It was good to get out of the café for a little bit. Being her first day, her mind was spinning with all that she had to learn. She found that she actually liked the busy work, liked that people asked her for things, and she could provide it. Bring a smile to their faces for something so simple as serving a meal, or fetching another drink.

She tried to forget about the woman on the phone who'd laughed at her. At least Silvia wouldn't be there when the woman came in. She set the box in the passenger seat of the SUV, then started the engine. It was hot and stifling inside, and she rolled down the window, then turned on the AC full blast.

The radio came on, preset to a country music station. Silvia didn't mind it, though it did remind her of Westin. But she was in Texas, and she'd just have to get used to country music without thinking of a certain bull rider all of the time.

Turning onto Main Street, she followed the signs to the rodeo arena. It wouldn't have been too hard to find, anyway. This town was small enough to spit across. Silvia winced. She'd heard Westin say that on the day they'd met. Now it appeared he was in her head.

The radio switched to a song about some cowboy crooning to his lost love. Silvia punched the button to switch stations. Another country station with a lady singing about forgiving her man. Time to listen to the Texas wind—she shut off the radio just as the arena came into sight.

Memories stuttered through her—of that night Westin won the bull riding, of their conversation in the parking lot, of how she'd put her number into his phone.

Silvia turned the AC up one more notch, then pulled into the parking lot, where a couple of trucks were parked and a group of guys were painting a small building, which must be the ticket booth. Shirtless.

Oh, boy.

It was fine. One of them was Mariah's *brother*, and she didn't care who the other guys were. As far as Silvia was concerned, she was on a hiatus from dating—for a long, long time.

She parked behind one of the trucks, which looked familiar, but as long as it wasn't red, Silvia was good. Leaving the engine—and the AC—running, she climbed out, then walked around the front to the passenger side.

Two of the cowboys had turned. She didn't recognize them. One was a skinny redhead, probably Mariah's brother, and the other had dark hair and a bit more heft. Their bare torsos left little to the imagination. The other two guys continued painting and didn't look over.

The one with the brown hair looked familiar—at least his profile did. Maybe she'd seen him about town.

And the fourth—her stomach knotted.

Because just as she reached the passenger door and opened it, he turned, paintbrush in hand.

From her first meeting with Westin Farr, she knew he was in shape. A t-shirt and jeans and a big ole cowboy hat couldn't hide that fact. And on one level, she knew that any guy who rode livestock for sport had to be muscular in many places. All places, in fact. Now she could see for herself that any fantasy she'd ever allowed herself to have of Westin Farr was absolutely true.

And he was now staring at her from beneath that dang cowboy hat of his.

She forced her gaze to drop, and she tugged open the door, then leaned into the cooler interior to grab the box of food. She let the AC blow on her very hot face for a few seconds before she moved. What were the chances of Westin Farr still being in Lost Creek, and *here,* building a ticket booth at the rodeo grounds? Apparently, very high.

And now she had the image of his shirtless torso seared into her brain. Those muscled shoulders, that six-pack, which actually might be an eight. But she wasn't counting. Or noticing his low-slung jeans. The tawny gold of his skin, which told her he didn't always wear a shirt when he was outside.

And those dark green eyes that she was pretty sure were still looking at her.

"Can I carry that for you, ma'am?" a deep voice said.

Silvia yelped and turned. Ryan Prosper. Now she recognized him. The heat must have been making her a little foggy in the head.

"Uh . . ." She could certainly get out of here faster if he helped. "That would be great. I put in some cookies, too. On the house. I thought you boys could use some extra food in this hot sun . . ." She was absolutely babbling.

Ryan nodded, his blue eyes friendly. "Thank you. That was real thoughtful of you, ma'am."

He was a very nice specimen to look at as well, but Silvia wasn't looking, not when Westin Farr was now walking toward her.

"Smells amazing," the redhead said as Ryan delivered food.

"Must be my lucky day," the other guy said, lifting one of the wrapped containers out of the box.

Silvia shut the passenger door and moved quickly around the rear of the SUV. Maybe Westin would stop at the food box with the other guys. Pick up his own plate. Nope. He was still coming.

She reached the driver's side and opened the door, but before she could slip inside, Westin grasped the top of it. Stopping her from her shutting the door and escaping.

"How are you?" he said, in a low voice that the other guys couldn't hear.

She tried to look everywhere but at him and his eyes, or his shoulders, or his chest.

"Fine." It came out as a whisper. How embarrassing. She lifted her chin and met his gaze head on. "Thanks for asking. Looks like you're keeping busy. Better eat that food before it gets cold."

But he didn't move, his gaze somehow keeping her captive. "I don't think that food's gonna cool down anytime soon. It's gotta be ninety degrees out here."

Her gaze betrayed her then. It strayed from his eyes, to his shoulders and chest. "Um, at least." She swallowed. Then she saw the bruising on his shoulder. "That looks rough."

He glanced down, then shrugged. "Just part of rodeo."

Well, if he didn't care, then she wasn't going to care for him. "I should go."

He nodded, and she slipped into the driver's seat, but his hand was still gripping the door.

"I was right pleased to hear that you're continuing with the barbeque sauce," Westin said. "Kellie told me—hope you don't mind."

Silvia could only shake her head.

He continued as if he had all day to make conversation. "I guess the distributor meeting went well?"

Right. That. "Yeah, it went better than I had expected. He's, uh, putting money into supplies and everything."

Westin's mouth curved.

Dang. She loved that smile of his.

"Good news, darlin'," he said. "I'm not surprised. Your sauce is amazing, and everyone should be able to enjoy it."

Darlin'. She'd told him not to call her that. Of course, it was probably an inborn habit of his. Reality slammed back into her. She wasn't going to be swayed by pretty talk from a good-looking cowboy. "Thanks again. I've really got to go."

Westin stepped back and touched the brim of his hat.

Silvia pulled the door shut, then tried to focus on backing up without looking at the cowboy standing in the middle of the parking lot, gazing after her. As she drove back to the café, her hands shook. She was over Westin, she was. She just had to remind her heart of that fact.

Chapter 22

"Mom took a fall," Cheryl told Westin on the phone.

He closed his eyes, and the worst-case scenarios tumbled through his mind. "What happened? Did she break anything?"

"She was carrying tomato starts out to the garden and slipped on the porch steps," Cheryl said. "They did an x-ray at the ER. Her ankle is broken at the very least, and the ER doctor said she'll need surgery. Without an MRI, he wasn't sure about the ligaments. We have an appointment with an orthopedic surgeon in a couple of hours to make a decision."

Westin exhaled. "Is she in pain?"

"They gave her something for it," Cheryl said.

"All right." Westin looked over at Ryan and the crew, who were nearly finished painting the ticket booth. "I can look up flights right now, but the next one won't leave until tomorrow morning if I want only one connection." He knew this from experience.

"Don't you have a rodeo or something? I don't really know when her surgery will be."

"There's always a rodeo," Westin said. "I can pull out of the upcoming one. I don't want to leave everything to you."

"I'm fine, West," Cheryl said. "And Mom will be fine, eventually. You don't need to come all the way back again. You were just here."

Cheryl could handle it, he knew that. But staying here just didn't sit right. Surgery wasn't anything to sniff at. Besides, Cheryl had her kid, and her husband had crazy working hours. "I'll look up flights all the same. Keep me posted, please."

"Will do," Cheryl said.

"Can I talk to her?"

"Of course," Cheryl said. "Hang on."

A few minutes later, his mom's voice came on the phone. "Did you hear about my gymnastics stunt?"

Westin chuckled. It was just like his mom to turn it into a joke. "Aren't you too old for gymnastics?"

"Haven't you heard that sixty is the new forty?"

Westin smiled. "Next time you miss me that much, just tell me I need to stay longer."

"Funny, son. But don't you dare come back," his mom said. "Cheryl is stressing me out enough."

"Is that right?"

"Sit here, Mom; put your leg up, Mom; drink this, Mom; do you need help to the bathroom, Mom? It's exhausting."

Westin laughed. "You did the same thing when I broke my arm in sixth grade."

"Well, you were a rambunctious little boy who wouldn't sit still, and the doctor said if you fell again, you'd make it worse."

Westin nodded, remembering. Ironically, he'd fallen off a mechanical bull. "Yeah, but you didn't have to be so bossy all the time."

"I did, and you know it."

Westin was grinning. "All right, Mom. You're right. And I'll see you tomorrow."

"Westin, I said—"

"Here's the thing, Mom. I'm an adult now, and I can fly home to see my mother anytime."

She gave a soft sigh. "All right, son. Safe travels. And I love you."

"Love you, too."

After hanging up, he rejoined the guys and began to paint again.

"Everything okay?" Ryan asked.

Westin filled him in, then said, "Mind if I crash at your place tonight? It will keep me out of trouble."

"Trouble meaning, away from the woman who delivered our lunch?"

"Yep."

"Sounds like a plan," Ryan said. "Lars is coming into town tonight sometime."

"Oh, nice. Saw him last night at the rodeo, and I wondered if he was sticking around, but we didn't get to that part of the conversation."

"Yeah, he doesn't want to go back to Montana for a while," Ryan said. "Guess he's going to follow the circuits closer to Lost Creek, even though he says the heat will be the death of him."

Westin laughed. Both he and Ryan probably looked like they'd just walked out of a lake.

Westin knew Lars had issues with his brother, who was the ranch manager at his family place in Montana. Lars would work there off and on, saving up for his own ranch someday. But at thirty, it was taking longer than he'd planned. Riding rodeo helped bring in the money, but only when he came out on top.

By the time they were finished with the ticket booth, Westin was proud of the day's work. It had kept him busy, exhausted him physically, but did little to take his mind off Silvia. Part of that could be due to the fact that she'd shown up with lunch.

Pretty as a picture.

Her dark eyes looking at him as if she was torn between talking to him or leaving... She'd talked a little, so maybe they wouldn't be complete strangers. Friends might be a stretch, but he wouldn't mind friends. Although he still hoped for more. He hadn't exactly seen forgiveness in her eyes, but the anger wasn't there anymore. Maybe he could hope.

Back at Ryan's place, Westin's shower was cold, as needed, and then he stayed busy putting together dinner on his own while Ryan left for a few hours to spend time with his lady. Westin had booked a morning flight, and would arrive before his mom went into surgery, so that took some of his worry away.

Before Westin sat down to eat, a truck pulled up in front of the house. He stood and saw Lars climbing out of his truck, so Westin walked onto the porch to greet him.

Lars looked like he hadn't slept recently. His plaid shirt was untucked, and his eyes had violet circles beneath them. When he pulled his hat off inside, he scrubbed a hand through his auburn hair. "Smells good."

"Hungry?"

"Starving."

Westin chuckled. "Follow me. Made some taco salad."

Lars walked in behind Westin and stopped in the kitchen. "You call that taco salad?"

Westin glanced at the plate he'd made of meat, beans, tomatoes, cheese, and lettuce. "Yeah?"

"Looks like garbage surprise," Lars said, moving into the kitchen and finding his own plate.

"But it tastes like heaven."

Lars smirked, then he piled food onto his plate and took the first bite. "All right, I take it back. This is good."

"Or you're starving."

Lars shrugged. "That, too."

"What's up?" Westin said after a few minutes of eating. "Ryan said there's trouble in Big Sky land?"

Lars took a sip of his drink, then said, "Nothing new, really. Same old story with my brother. He's gonna run my parents' ranch into the ground, and he won't listen to any reason." He met Westin's gaze. "You never called. What's up with your woman?"

"Ex-woman," Westin said. "Is there such a thing?"

"What happened?"

Westin told him about her silent treatment, his all-night drive, how he went on a jog in his cowboy boots, followed by her speaking her mind—not holding back a thing. "And that's it."

Lars leaned back in his chair and folded his arms. "You don't look like a dying man with a heart bleeding all over the road. Was she just a fling?"

"No," Westin shot out. He rubbed his chin. "Sorry."

Lars still waited.

"I saw her this afternoon, and we chatted," he said. "I don't think she hates me that much."

"Just a little?"

Westin smirked. "And now I'm heading home tomorrow. My mom's having surgery."

"Ah, what happened?"

Westin filled him in, then they spent the next hour reminiscing about some of their college antics and rodeo events. Those were definitely great days, but the future was what Westin was looking forward to. And he hoped that Silvia would be in it. She'd talked to him when she'd delivered lunch, and the anger had been gone from her eyes. He was going to hold onto that for now.

CHAPTER 23

IT HAD BEEN THREE days since Silvia had seen Westin Farr. Not that she was looking for him, and not that she expected him to still be in Lost Creek. He'd come back, after all, to confront her. So what was here that he should stay for?

But as she drove another delivery to the rodeo grounds, where some guys had ordered food while they were training or something, she was half-hoping, and half-dreading, that Westin would be among them.

He wasn't.

She delivered the barbeque chicken plates with no intrusive questions or shirtless men stopping her from leaving right away.

Her days were busy, thankfully, and her distributor had been delivering better and better news every day. She had more orders coming in from surrounding towns. In fact, she'd need to hire some help if this all kept up.

She thought of the women at the ranch, and whether any of them would be interested in sticking around in Lost Creek and working for her. Maybe she could approach Kellie to see what she thought of each woman's potential.

When Silvia reached the café, she nearly slammed on the brakes of Mariah's SUV. There was a crowd in front of the café. Was there a lunch special going on? Silvia sensed they weren't there for her barbeque sauce—because people were surrounding a guy with dark hair and a Sharks baseball cap.

Axel.

Her brother was here.

Kellie wasn't supposed to tell him anything for at least a week. Not until Silvia was better settled.

But apparently, he'd found out.

Silvia pulled behind the café and parked, then she went in the back door and up the stairs to her rented room. She wasn't going to face her brother in public. No, he could find her here, and then they'd have a talk that was way past due.

Yeah, she'd ignored his texts and phone calls the past several days. But she'd done that at the women's ranch, too.

Fifteen minutes later, she heard the footsteps coming up the stairs outside of her door. Then someone knocked.

"Silv?" Axel said through the door. "You in there?"

She exhaled. "Come in. It's unlocked."

The doorknob turned, then Axel stepped into the small room. It seemed half the size with him standing inside of it.

She expected anger in his dark eyes, or maybe hurt, but instead, she saw only wariness.

"Hi," he said, his tone careful. "The lady downstairs said I could come up. Mariah? I hope that's okay?"

Well, this was new.

Silvia crossed her legs on her bed, where she was sitting. "Have a seat." She pointed to the only chair in the room.

Axel took a seat, his larger presence still dominating the room, although he was more quiet than she ever remembered him being.

"Mariah told me about your barbeque sauce getting orders from other places as well."

Silvia nodded, waiting for the rush of words and advice. "She insisted I try some."

Silvia blinked in surprise.

"It's fantastic," he continued. "But you've always been an excellent cook."

Again, she was surprised. Had her brother ever told her that before? "Thanks."

He nodded, then he leaned forward and linked his hands together. His dark eyes focused on her, and she noticed new, tired lines about his face. "Here's the thing, Silv. I only want you to be happy."

Dang. She was going to cry. This wasn't the time.

"And I can see now that I've made things difficult for you," he said. "Those books showed me a lot of things I've messed up on."

Her eyes burned.

"I've taken some things to the extreme when I should have backed off," he said, his voice soft. "Let you make mistakes, even fail once in a while. Because that's how we grow and become who we're supposed to be. Heck, I've screwed up more times than I can count in baseball and college, yet they were mistakes *I* could own."

Silvia wiped at an escaped tear.

"I hope you can forgive me," he said. "Someday. This is going to be a big change, and I'm trying, but I'm going to probably screw up another time or two."

"More than that."

Axel's eyes widened, then he smiled. "You're right. More than that."

She drew in a shaky breath. "Thanks for apologizing. And I hope you can forgive me, too."

His brows tugged together. "For what?"

"For being difficult."

"You were going through some hard things—"

Silvia raised a hand. "Believe me, I knew when I was being difficult, and sometimes it was just to get under your skin."

His brows popped up. "Really?"

Silvia's smile was tentative. "Yeah."

His mouth quirked. "Okay, then. Good to know."

A moment passed, then two.

"I also wanted to tell you that Brighton is pregnant."

Silvia stared at her brother. He and his wife had been trying for a couple of years, and now . . . She leapt to her feet. "Oh, my gosh. That's so great!" She hugged him, nearly knocking him out of his chair.

Axel pulled her close and held her tight. "She's through the first trimester. She didn't want to give anyone false hope."

Brighton was another person Silvia had been ignoring, and now she felt that surge of guilt. But this could be rectified. She drew away from Axel. "How is she feeling? Is she sick?"

"Mostly tired," he said. "But she's doing good so far. We have our first ultrasound next week."

Silvia settled back onto her bed. "I can't believe it. So, she's due when?"

Axel actually blushed. It was adorable. "Around Halloween."

"Aww." Her tears were replaced by grinning.

"Now, tell me about your barbeque sauce business," Axel said. "I promise to just listen and not take over."

Silvia laughed. "That will be the day." But she told him. Everything. And it felt good, and normal, and somehow healing.

When she finished, Axel wiped at his eyes. "I'm so proud of you, sis."

Silvia blinked back her own tears. "Well, maybe I did

learn something from my brother. How to negotiate a contract."

He chuckled, then an alert went off on his phone, and he looked at it. "I hate to say this, but I've gotta go. I have a game tonight, so I used Cole's private jet to get here, but I only had an hour."

"Where can I get a friend who owns a jet?" Silvia teased. Cole Hunter was a pro-baseball player and a close friend to Axel. They'd played college together with the Belltown Six Pack gang, which included Grizz McCarthy. Cole made a decent salary in the MLB, of course, but his real money came from his father's oil empire.

"You know Cole would help you out anytime," Axel said, rising to his feet.

Silvia rose, too. "I know." She hugged her brother again, and for the first time in a long time, she was grateful to be with him. Things had changed between them. She could feel it. He was giving her space, he was respecting her, and he was finally proud of her.

But more importantly, she didn't need his accolades. Not anymore.

Axel headed to the door and opened it, but before walking into the hall, he said, "Oh, by the way, I had a talk with that cowboy of yours."

"He's not mine."

Axel's eyes narrowed. "You broke up with him?"

Silvia folded her arms. Talking to her brother about men she dated was something she didn't want to do right now. "Something like that."

Axel rubbed a hand over his chin. "Well, I guess what I was going to say no longer matters, then."

"Wait." Silvia crossed the room. "What were you going to say?"

Axel dropped his hand. "He was the first guy who stood up to me about you. Didn't back down, either. Said the relationship was between the two of you. He wasn't cowed in the least when I threatened him."

Silvia tamped down her anger. "You threatened him?"

Her brother at least had the decency to look abashed. "He's definitely his own man and knows his own mind. When all was said and done, I was impressed. Although I don't really approve of him going behind my back and dating you."

"I'm an adult," Silvia said in an even tone.

He chuckled. "Yeah, that's what he said. And if you change your mind, I won't put up a fuss. As long as he keeps in line, of course."

Silvia had no words. This was all too much, but too late. It didn't change anything, did it? No. Westin had gone behind her back with her brother.

His phone chimed again. "Well, I really should go." His gaze settled on her. "Love you."

"Love you, too. Tell Brighton hi from me. And Mom, of course."

"Sure thing."

After her brother left, it was a long time before Silvia left her room and headed down to the café. She had a lot to think about, but mostly, she was grateful for this new beginning with her brother. It didn't change her mind about staying in Lost Creek and working on this new business, but it made her heart feel ten times lighter.

And the news about Brighton was thrilling. Silvia would be an auntie.

Her phone buzzed with a text, and Silvia picked it up. It was from Glory.

Hey, hon. Thought I'd see if you're around. I'm heading out and wanted to say goodbye.

Silvia frowned. *You're done at the ranch?*

Yep. Been six weeks, and now it's time for new horizons. What are your plans?

Selling my house to get rid of memories, and then I'm going to wander the globe in search of the meaning of life.

Classic Glory. Silvia laughed and wrote back. *Perfect. I'm coming, too.*

I wouldn't complain, Glory wrote back.

Silvia sighed. Maybe someday she'd have a carefree spirit like Glory.

Silvia checked her appearance in her mirror and smoothed back her hair into a ponytail, then fixed the mascara that had smeared with her crying. When she reached the café kitchen, things seemed to have slowed down. Apparently, the autograph seekers hadn't turned into buying customers.

"How did it go with your brother?" Mariah asked, turning from the oven, where she'd just taken out a freshly baked chicken pot pie. "He's a lot more handsome in person."

Silvia smiled, since she knew Mariah was only teasing and not one of those women who was trying to make a connection with him. "Good, and his wife is pregnant. So I'll get to be a proud auntie in a few months."

"Oh, wow, that's great," Mariah said. "He's welcome here anytime."

"I'll let him know that." She grabbed a clean cloth and wet it in the sink. "Want me to wipe down tables?"

"That would be great," Mariah said.

"Silvia?"

She turned to see a man on the other side of the register. A cowboy who she recognized, but wasn't exactly sure of his name. She was pretty sure he was one of the Lost Creek guys who'd come to the women's ranch for dinner that one night.

"Lars Jackson."

Ah. Lars. "That's right," she said. "And yeah, I'm Silvia."

Lars nodded, his hazel eyes quietly assessing her. And then Silvia remembered. Westin had told her Lars was who'd he'd talked to about Axel and that whole mess. Now, she suddenly felt self-conscious.

But she lifted her chin, kept ahold of his gaze. "Can I get you something from the menu?"

His gaze flickered. "How about one of your barbeque plate lunches? West says they're to die for."

Silvia nodded and moved to the register. Her neck was heating up at his mention of Westin, and she hoped it wouldn't spread to her cheeks. "Great. Anything to drink?"

"I'll take an orange soda."

She nodded without looking at him, and rang up the price. After he paid, Mariah started to prepare the barbeque plate, so Silvia remained in the front area.

No one else was in the café, so it was only her and Lars.

Dang. Would he try to talk to her about West?

She cleared some garbage from one of the tables, then wiped up the crumbs.

Lars remained by the register, waiting for his order. Thankfully, the music playing at the café kept things from being too awkward. Until . . . he said, "You know, if you don't mind me sayin', West agonized over what to do about your brother's texts."

Silvia paused and slowly looked over at the cowboy. He was leaning against the counter, his eyes on her.

"West and I aren't seeing each other anymore," she said point blank. "It's not a topic I'm willing to discuss with you or anyone else."

Could Mariah please hurry?

Lars didn't seem taken aback, or offended. He merely gave a small nod. "I understand. I thought you should know he was telling you the truth."

Silvia sighed and scrubbed a little harder at a ketchup spill that had dried on the table. "I know he was telling the truth, *after* the fact." She hadn't meant to say that. She didn't want anything getting back to West.

Great. Now Lars was walking toward her.

"Here's the thing, ma'am," Lars said. "I'm a guy who usually minds my own business, unless it's something that needs to be corrected. Westin Farr is about as honest as they come. Whatever went through his mind, it wasn't meant to hurt you. In fact, I reckon it was the opposite."

Silvia blinked.

"With all he's got going on, I just wanted to go on the record and give my two cents about his true character."

She didn't know what to think. Yeah, so maybe she'd attacked his character, but he'd been in the wrong. Even he'd admitted that. But something bothered her. "What do you mean, with all that he's got going on?"

Lars hesitated. "He's back in Oklahoma for his mom's surgery. And there was some scuttlebutt about his last rodeo ride at Mount Palmer and his score, so his win was stripped. He's got to earn that back at the Prosper rodeo this weekend, and he's determined to do that despite his shoulder injury."

Silvia stared. She'd seen the bruising on his shoulder that he'd brushed off when she'd commented. But the rest was new information to her. What was his mom's surgery for?

"Order's ready," Mariah said, coming out of the kitchen. She set the order on the counter. "To-go, right?"

"That's right," Lars said, his attention shifting to Mariah. "Thank you, ma'am."

Mariah smiled and headed back to the kitchen.

Before Silvia could question Lars, he said, "Have a good day, Miss Diaz." He touched the brim of his hat, then was out the door.

The bell above the door jangled with his departure, but Silvia barely had time to comprehend all that Lars had said before the bell rang again.

Glory swept in, all smiles and sad eyes. Her silver dangly earrings matched the jewelry at her neck and wrists, and she smelled like she'd overdone the perfume.

"I can't believe you're leaving," Silvia said, feeling teary-eyed. How many times was she going to cry today?

"Was that Lars I saw walking out of here?"

"It was," Silvia said. If anyone at the women's ranch knew most of her story with West, it was Glory. So with Mariah still busy in the kitchen, Silvia updated Glory on both what Lars had said and her brother.

"Oh, hon," Glory said, grasping her hand. "It sounds like Westin is waiting for you, just like he said. Him standing up to your brother like that is good stuff in my opinion."

Silvia smiled, although nerves were making her heart drum.

"Who's going to keep my head on straight after you leave?" she asked.

"You'll be fine, hon." Glory took out a pink tissue from her bright orange purse and dabbed at her eyes. "But I would like to see one more rodeo before I go back to my reality. What do you say we go to the Prosper one together? Isn't that this weekend?"

Silvia frowned. Lars had just mentioned that Westin would be riding at Prosper. "I don't really want Westin to think—"

"He doesn't even have to know we're there," Glory cut in. "It will be just us girls—our last rodeo, so to speak."

The idea was beginning to settle. "You'd stick around for that?"

"Sure," Glory said. "I'll get a spot at the bed and breakfast and help you make barbeque sauce for the next couple of days."

Silvia couldn't turn down an offer like that, even if it did mean she'd be watching Westin bull riding again. "It's a deal."

Chapter 24

"Good luck, son," Westin's mom had told him before he left Oklahoma. "Keep riding. We're fine here."

It was an age-old argument that had started when his father passed away. Westin had left the circuit so he could go home and run the ranch. But his mom and his sister had demanded that he stay in rodeo. So, they'd hired a cousin to be the ranch manager, but Dustin was in his mid-sixties now, and he'd eventually want to retire and focus on his own place.

Now, as Westin pulled into the small town of Prosper, memories assailed him. He'd come here with his dad more than once, and his dad had always won the bull riding here.

Westin hoped to pay that homage.

Not to mention rectify the nastiness that was circulating about corrupt scoring in that last rodeo in Mount Palmer. Westin hated that type of controversy. A cowboy and his livestock should be a straight-up competition.

Still, Westin had already sent back his prize money, and chalked it up to avoiding that town again. He wouldn't be surprised if Mr. Palmer was behind some of this—the crooked guy.

Westin didn't bother with the bed and breakfast—it was

probably booked out, anyway. He'd sleep in or under his truck tonight, depending on the temperature. As he pulled up to the rodeo grounds, his phone came to life with texts as if on cue. There must be a cell pod close by.

He parked, then looked at his phone.

The Chute was making predictions about the Prosper Rodeo tonight.

Westin read a text from Eric: *I'm coming to interview you. Save me five minutes.*

Are you bringing the makeup kit? Reid asked.

For you, always, Eric replied.

I'm gonna put twenty on West, Lars cut in.

Reid: *West? Who's that? Knox is gonna win it all. It's his hometown.*

But West has some payback to do after Mount Palmer, Lars continued.

Then why only twenty? West chimed in. *How about a hundred?*

The numbers only escalated from there, and Westin laughed. He soon climbed out of the truck and headed to the arena office to check in. Old Man Prosper was there—well, he was Mayor Rex Prosper, technically.

"Well, well, well," the mayor boomed in that heavy voice of his, "if it isn't the Farr kid." He wore a pressed button-down, his signature tan Levi's, and of course, the belt buckle that read "Prosperity Ranch." It was said that the mayor polished his boots twice a day.

"Good to see you, sir," Westin said, shaking the man's thick hand.

"Sorry about your dad," Rex said. "I thought the world of him."

They shot the breeze for a few minutes, then Rex headed off to attend to some business. Westin gazed over the arena. It felt good to be in the heat and dirt again, and it felt good to be looking forward to the rodeo. Not much else took a man's full focus when he was trying to stay atop a bull. His shoulder felt pretty good. Almost an entire week staying away from any riding had done wonders.

"Good to see ya," someone called out as he headed to his truck.

Westin turned to see Knox Prosper, who was leaner and more wiry than Westin remembered him. Knox was leaning against his truck, talking to a pretty redhead who looked quite cozy with him.

Knox had been married at one point. Westin had heard about his divorce, and he was 99.9% sure this wasn't his ex-wife.

"How's it goin'?"

"Can't complain," Knox said. "Jana, this is Westin Farr, my main competition tonight. West, this is Jana Harris. My sweetheart."

She flushed nearly the color of her hair.

Westin smiled. "Nice to meet you. I'll see y'all later tonight." He tipped his hat. He had no interest hanging around the lovey-dovey couple. Not when his heart was still in shutdown mode.

He was going to find a place to shower, grab some grub, then focus on earning some of his lost cash tonight. And he'd have to take out Knox Prosper again to do it.

Four hours later, Westin returned to the rodeo arena, where the parking lot was now half-full with arriving spectators. He was about to do something that he'd put off as long as possible, but now, it was time to be a friend to Eric.

And . . . there he was. Eric waved and strode over. He was all pimped up—well as much as a cowboy from Wyoming could be. A nicer navy shirt, clean jeans, and his hat looked new, too. Oh, and his boots were polished. Not that they'd stay that way for long.

"West, I thought you'd be hiding in the stands like a chicken."

Westin laughed and bro-hugged Eric, clapping him on the back. He felt a twinge in his shoulder, but ignored it. "You'd just hunt me down anyway, maybe send one of the rodeo clowns to look."

Eric grinned. "All right. Let's get this thing going. Five minutes, okay? My audience has a life, you know, so I keep them short and sweet."

"Whatever," Westin teased, although he was surprisingly nervous.

They walked over by the bullpens, where Eric found a place to stand. He turned on this camera contraption, then did the introduction that Westin had heard more than once, since he'd watched some of the episodes out of obligation.

"This is Westin Farr, folks, son of the legendary Bud Farr," Eric said. "Keep your eye on Westin here, because he's making his own name for himself. Now, West, tell us why you decided to become a bull rider when there are many other, much safer, rodeo events."

That was an easy one, and as Westin explained, he found that talking on camera was easier than he thought—as long as it was something he was interested in. He talked about his growing up years on his family's ranch, and how his dad used to take him to rodeos.

"There I was, a kid of eight, watching my dad perform—riding the gnarliest beasts in the arena." Westin paused, the image clear in his mind of his father. Wearing the same hat Westin had on now, his body graceful and strong atop a bucking bull, his grin after a ride . . . "Well, I guess you could say I was born and raised in rodeo. And it helped that my mom was supportive, because if there's one thing a cowboy needs, it's his woman to—"

But then his voice faltered, and he lost his train of

thought when he caught a glimpse of a dark-haired woman who was the twin of Silvia Diaz. Could there be two of them in the world? The arena lights were blaring overhead as twilight turned to a deeper blue, so his eyes must be playing tricks on him.

"Well, it looks like Westin is already focusing on his upcoming event," Eric continued. "Until next time, cowboys and cowgirls."

Eric said in a more normal tone, "That was great, West. Thanks. I'll just have to edit some of the end where you stopped mid-sentence." He frowned. "You okay?"

Westin looked at Eric, away from the people entering the arena. "Yeah, fine. Just thought I saw someone I knew. Thanks for the interview. See you after?"

"Yeah, sure—"

Westin strode away before Eric could ask any more questions. He headed right into the group of people who'd just handed over their tickets. If that woman had been Silvia, she couldn't have gotten far. He scanned the stands for a dark-haired woman with a black hat and sky-blue shirt.

It took him only a moment.

She was here.

He had to be seeing things, right? But no, he recognized the woman she was with—spunky woman in her '50s, short hair, pink cowboy hat—from the women's ranch. Two cowboys were talking to them, flirting as if their lives depended on it.

Glory laughed at something the men said, but Silvia seemed distracted. Her gaze shifted from the cowboys and seemed to be searching the arena. For *him*?

Did she know he was here tonight, competing? His heart betrayed him with hope.

There was only one way to find out. He took the stairs

heading up the stands two at a time until he reached Silvia's row.

She saw him at the same time Glory did.

"Well, if it isn't Westin Farr," Glory said, her voice sounding expectant.

Silvia's gaze lingered on him for a second, then she looked away.

"If I'd known you ladies were coming, I'd have gotten you better seats."

Again, Silvia glanced at him. He wished he knew what was going through her mind.

"You Westin Farr?" one of the cowboys said. "Honored to meet you."

"Nice to meet you, too," Westin said. Then he went out on a limb. "Do you mind if I talk to the ladies here for a minute?"

"Sure thing," the other cowboy said, and they moved a few feet away.

Both women were looking at him now. Glory's eyes were sparkling with humor, and Silvia's . . . it was too hard to read hers.

"You drove all the way to Prosper?" he said.

"Sure did," Glory supplied, since Silvia still hadn't said anything. "Our last girls' night out together. I'm heading home tomorrow."

Glory continued to talk about things that Westin was hardly paying attention to.

Why was Silvia so quiet? What was going through that pretty head of hers?

The arena was filling up, and a group of people excused themselves to get past Glory and Silvia.

He should go. Soon. Right now. Or else he'd be subjected to Glory's future plans, it seemed.

"Nice to see you, ladies," he said with a nod. "Enjoy the show."

"Oh, we will," Glory said.

Another glance at Silvia, and he turned to leave.

"West," she said, her voice soft, but he heard it loud and clear.

He turned, his pulse picking up speed. "Yeah?" He almost said *darlin'*, but had to hold it back.

"I talked to Lars," she said.

She didn't offer anything more, but the way she was looking at him was . . . like she wasn't angry anymore.

A heartbeat passed, then two.

"And I talked to Axel," she said. "He knows about my business, and he told me . . . what you told him."

Westin hated that they were surrounded by people. He even hated that Glory was hearing this, because Silvia wasn't telling him something casual. It was significant, and he wanted to understand more. Ask her questions. But here, and now, wasn't the place.

Silvia had the tiniest smile curving her lips.

He swallowed against the dryness of his throat. "If you ladies don't have plans after, maybe we could grab a bite to eat together?"

Glory agreed immediately, but it was Silvia's answer that he was listening for.

When she said, "That would be nice," he nearly grabbed her and whooped.

Instead, he nodded. "See you after, then."

It took every ounce of his strength to head down those arena stairs like nothing earth-shattering had just happened. Silvia was talking to him. She was reconsidering. He could feel it to the depths of his bones.

Nothing would stop him from winning tonight. Nothing.

CHAPTER 25

SILVIA SHOULD BE USED to watching Westin bull ride by now, but something wasn't right. She couldn't explain how she knew. He was hanging on to the fiercely bucking bull named Little Sprite—which must be a joke of a name. But Westin's expression was gritted... in pain?

The eight-second buzzer rang, and the crowd went wild. Instead of scrambling away from the bull, though, Westin was slow to move. And that's when it happened.

In a flurry of hooves that seemed to move in slow motion, the bull stepped on Westin's chest, more than once.

Silvia gasped.

The crowd went dead silent. The music died off.

Cowboys jumped into the arena, some of them herding the bull away, and others kneeling at Westin's side.

"No, no, no," Silvia whispered.

Glory gripped her arm, muttering a prayer.

When the stretcher came out, Silvia began to cry. It wasn't something she could control or hold back, it was like her body had a mind of its own. Glory's arms went around her, and they watched in horror as Westin was carted out of the arena. He lifted a hand and waved, which brought cheers from the crowd.

"Does that mean he's okay?" Silvia asked no one in particular. "Please be okay, please."

The MC came on, assuring that Westin Farr was in good hands, and they'd update the crowd when news came back. Meanwhile, another bull rider prepared to go out next, but Silvia felt sick to her stomach. She couldn't stay here and watch anymore.

Westin had to be in pain, and what if . . . what if something was crushed or he was paralyzed?

"I need to get out of here," she told Glory.

"Of course, hon," she soothed. "You don't look so good."

"I can't breathe very well."

They didn't make it out of the arena before Silvia had to sit down. Glory asked some people to move over in the front row, then told Silvia to put her head down.

"Focus on breathing, hon," Glory said, rubbing Silvia's back. "Is this one of those panic attacks you told us about?"

Silvia couldn't even answer; she was close to throwing up. It was as if she was frozen in place, her muscles locked.

Dimly, she heard someone else say, "Is she okay? Should we get the medics?"

"She'll be fine," came Glory's steady voice. "Just needs to sit for a bit."

How could Glory be so calm? How could they just sit here when Westin was possibly dying?

The crowd was cheering for one of the events, but Silvia had no idea which one, because she could only hear her own rapid thoughts.

Then the announcer's voice came on, mentioning Westin Farr.

She managed to lift her head, sure her tears had ruined every bit of makeup she'd applied.

"We got ourselves an update from the doc," the MC said. "Westin Farr is gonna be just fine, folks. A couple of broken ribs, that's all. Won't be surprised if we see him back real soon."

The crowd clapped at the news, and Silvia only wanted to curl up in a ball somewhere, but at least she was breathing easier now.

"When you feel up to it, we'll head to my car," Glory said. She'd brought her car to the women's recovery ranch because she only lived a couple of hours away from Lost Creek. "Want some of my water?"

Silvia gratefully accepted it. After drinking, she said, "Let's go. I think I'm okay now." She wasn't, but she could walk. She had to.

Hanging onto Glory, Silvia made it out of the arena without losing it again. The air was cooler in the parking lot, the noise less, and the lights not so bright. It all helped.

"Here we are," Glory said as she opened the passenger door to her car and ushered Silvia in. "You can just relax now on the drive home. Take a nap if you want to."

"I need to see him," Silvia said.

Glory paused before shutting the door. "Westin?"

"Yeah. Can you find out where they took him? I need to make sure he's all right. See it for myself."

Glory bit her lip, then said, "Sure thing, hon. I'll go see what I can find out."

Silvia leaned her head back on the seat and closed her eyes as she waited for Glory to return. She'd never felt such sickening fear in all her life. It was like the grand mal of panic attacks, and she'd been taking her meds regularly, too, so now she had something else to worry about.

When Glory returned, she said, "He's at the clinic down the road. Said it was the only medical clinic in town. A small town like this one, it shouldn't be too hard to find."

"Okay, great. Thank you."

"No problem."

Glory pulled out of the parking lot, then drove to the main street. With each passing moment, Silvia felt calmer. She had to be. Walking into the clinic like a mad woman wouldn't be a good thing.

Westin was the one who was hurt, not her.

She wondered what this would mean for his next rodeos. Would he take a month off, maybe longer? Would he go back to Oklahoma for a while?

Why should it matter to her? It did, that was all.

When Glory parked in front of a small building that said simply, "Prosper Medical Clinic," Silvia already had her hand on the door handle. She was out the second the car came to a stop.

Glory hurried behind her, and when Silvia stepped into the bright light of the clinic, she realized she probably looked a mess. Crying would have ruined all of her makeup. She'd hardly worn it in Lost Creek, but tonight, she'd decided to put more effort into her appearance. Little good that had done now.

"Can I help you?" a matronly woman with iron-gray hair and a pink scrub top asked from where she sat at the reception desk.

"Is Westin Farr here?"

The woman nodded. "Sure is, dear. You his . . ." She paused. "Wife?"

"Friend," Silvia said, then she realized she might not be allowed to see him if she wasn't a relative.

But apparently, a small town clinic didn't have such hang-ups.

"Follow me." The woman rose from her chair.

"I'll just wait here," Glory said, taking a seat in the lobby.

The receptionist led Silvia past the desk and down a short hallway. "He's in room three."

The door was ajar, and all seemed quiet inside. Maybe he was asleep?

After the receptionist left, Silvia pushed open the door slowly.

The first thing she saw was the exam table, and atop it was Westin. He was looking at his phone, his head turned away from her. She'd expected his ribs to be taped or something. But they weren't. His shirt was off, and he had a blue icepack strapped to one side.

Relief flooded through her. He was all right. He was breathing, checking out something on his phone. Everything was normal.

She'd panicked for nothing.

Now, embarrassment washed over her.

Westin turned his head before she could decide if she should stay or slip away. "Silvia?" His voice was rougher, deeper.

"Hi," she said, and then dang it, her eyes filled with tears.

Westin's brow furrowed. "You okay?"

She laughed, despite her stupid tears. "I'm fine. *You're* the one in a medical clinic." She walked into the room and stopped a couple of feet away from him. "I was worried and wanted to make sure you're okay."

Westin's smile was soft. "A couple of ribs got a beating, but I'll be fine in a few weeks. Although they ordered me to get an MRI at the main hospital the next city over to look at my shoulder."

His left shoulder had been the one bothering him, she knew. And now she saw the evidence of that with the bruising discoloration on it.

She winced at the sight and moved closer. "That can't feel good."

Westin chuckled, then drew in a sharp breath. "Probably shouldn't laugh and torture my ribs. But not much feels good when you get trampled by a bull."

Her gaze trailed to his chest, then lower to the ice pack over his left ribs.

"Two on the left side," he said. "Nothing on the right."

She nodded, her eyes welling again.

He moved his hand and linked their fingers. "You okay, darlin'?"

Her breathing stuttered, and she curled her fingers around his. This man was something else, not just as a bull rider, but the way he put others before himself. Besides the warmth of his touch, the way he called her darlin' was enough to make a sensible woman swoon.

"I had another panic attack."

He lifted the ice pack from his ribs and pushed up from the table, wincing, then sat facing her. "Come here."

"I don't want to hurt you," she said.

He pulled her into his arms anyway, and she tentatively leaned into his embrace. He felt so warm, so alive, so male. She turned her head and nestled against his neck. He smelled like the rodeo, but she didn't mind.

"What happened?" he asked, his chin resting on the top of her head.

"When they carried you away on a stretcher, something inside of me just broke," she whispered against his skin. "I thought I could get out of the arena in time, but Glory had to find me a spot to sit down. I was preparing myself to throw up in front of hundreds of spectators."

"But you didn't?"

She could hear the smile in his voice. "No. Glory stayed with me. Kept people from intruding."

"Glory is a great woman," he murmured.

She nodded. "She found out where you were and drove me over here."

Westin pulled back a little so their gazes met. "Really. And you wanted to come here, because . . ."

A smile slipped out. "Because you said something about dinner, remember?"

"How could I forget, darlin'?" His brow creased. "Can I call you that?"

The warmth in her chest heated. "I'm thinking about it."

He smiled, his gaze soaking her in. "That's the best news I've had all week."

She was about two seconds from kissing him—how could she not? But her cell rang. Maybe Glory was tired of waiting.

"I should get that," she said, reluctantly stepping out of his arms and fishing the phone from her back pocket. When her mom's number showed up on the screen, Silvia frowned. Her mom went to bed religiously at eight p.m. every night when she was home because of her early mornings, and right now, it was after nine in Seattle.

"Hi, Mom," she said, turning slightly away from Westin, who was now holding the ice pack against his side.

"Silvia," her mom said. "They're at the hospital. Brighton might lose the baby."

Shock rippled through Silvia. "What? No, that can't happen! She's in her second trimester. Everything's supposed to be fine."

"I know," her mom said. "Axel just called, and I wasn't quite asleep because I was reading. He told me I could tell you."

Silvia closed her eyes. Exhaled. She hated to think of Brighton dealing with something so hard. She and Axel would be the most amazing parents—Axel could put all of his fatherly overprotectiveness to good use.

"I'm coming out," Silvia said. "I don't know how I'll get there yet, but I'll figure it out."

"Do you need my credit card?" her mom asked, and for a good reason, too.

In one of her fits before leaving Seattle, Silvia had cut up all of her bank cards and thrown them at Axel.

"No," she said. "I'm going to call Cole Hunter."

Well, her mother couldn't argue with that. No one could, really.

She hung up and found Westin staring at her.

"Bad news?"

Silvia told him about Axel's wife, and somehow, she held back the tears. "I'm going to call Cole, and hopefully, I can get to Seattle tonight."

"Cole Hunter, the baseball centerfielder?"

"Yeah. He has a private jet and said I can use it anytime. Well, this is that time."

Westin moved off the table and drew on his dirt-stained shirt. He winced more than once at his movements.

As Silvia waited for Cole to answer his phone, she said, "What are you doing?"

"I'm coming with you."

CHAPTER 26

IF WESTIN EVER HAD more money than he knew what to do with, he vowed that he would, indeed, buy a private jet.

This was livin'.

Thankfully, there'd been enough lead time to get a change of clothing from his truck, and change in the clinic. And it was quite comical as Silvia drove them to the airport. In his truck. She said she'd driven her brother's truck before, but Westin doubted that story.

Good thing the roads were mostly empty at midnight.

And now, they were racing across the night sky toward Seattle, surrounded by plush leather chairs, and no kidding—a full-size bathroom. Which, of course, Westin had used to shower.

He hoped the jet owner wouldn't mind.

It turned out Cole Hunter was in some sort of private jet club, so he didn't always need to send his jet to the rescue. He just booked whichever jet was available at the nearest airport.

What a life.

And now Westin was currently in his own bit of heaven. To his surprise, and immense pleasure, Silvia had taken the chair next to his. And within twenty minutes—after his shower and being restored to a clean-smelling man—she'd fallen asleep, her head on his good shoulder.

He wasn't planning on moving any time soon, anyway.

He didn't even know who won the bull riding tonight, and he didn't care. He'd be off the circuit for eight weeks minimum. Six to heal his ribs, and two more to get back up to par. And until then, he planned to see where this thing between him and Silvia was going.

He was pretty sure she'd forgiven him, even though she hadn't said those exact words. But her willingness to talk to him and agree to dinner at the rodeo, then her visit to the medical clinic, followed by virtually no fuss put up by her when he said he'd go with her to Seattle... those were all solid signs, right?

His phone buzzed with a text since the jet had Wi-Fi. He should probably turn the thing off. Slipping it out of his pocket, he glanced at the screen.

The Chute.

Of course. No time limits for them. One would be texting late at night, while another would start texting before dawn.

Eric had also called three times.

Oh. Well.

They were asking about his injury.

Whoops.

He continued scrolling, then his eyes nearly popped out at the next group of texts.

Eric: *Where did you go? You matched your dad's record, dude! You're now the third person in the entire world of bull riding who holds a perfect 100-point score. We all headed to the medical clinic to find you. Even Mayor Prosper wanted to congratulate you, but they said you'd left with a woman.*

Reid: *Wow, congrats, West. You're the man! I always knew you'd reach that record someday!*

Ford: *I owe you dinner. Name the time and place! Huge congrats!*

Ryan: *We're putting up a banner at Lost Creek arena in your honor. This is major, West. I know your dad's celebrating in heaven right now.*

Lars: *Congrats! What a stud. One question—who's the woman you left the clinic with?*

At least he'd texted his sister while in the medical clinic. She hadn't responded—but she'd see it in the morning and wouldn't have to worry if she heard the news from someone else. News traveled fast in the rodeo world. News about his injury, and now about his new record.

Westin wrote back a quick reply to his Lost Creek bros: *Thanks for letting me know about the record. I had no idea. So stoked. Went to the clinic. Two broken ribs. I'll be back on the circuit in eight weeks. I'm gonna get an MRI for my shoulder as well in a couple of days. Right now, I'm heading to Seattle with a friend. I'm taking you up on the dinner offer, Ford.*

The message group exploded with questions and GIFs.

Westin tried to keep his laughter at a minimum, first, because he didn't want to wake the sleeping beauty on his shoulder, and second, it really did hurt to laugh. In fact, he was in pain right now, but he still wasn't going to search out some ibuprofen and disturb Silvia.

When Westin confirmed that yes, he was with Silvia and they were going to Seattle together, but no, it wasn't anyone's business why and what was going on between the two of them... another series of texts and GIFs came through.

Westin sent a final thumbs-up, then turned off his phone.

He might have also dozed, because the next thing he knew, Silvia was tapping him on his good shoulder. "Wake up, cowboy. We're in a new town."

He opened his eyes, and the soft smile on Silvia's face went straight to his heart. She'd cleaned off the smudged mascara, and he decided that her no-makeup look was his favorite.

"Good morning," he said, his voice a rasp.

"If you call three in the morning good."

He leaned forward, because he was aiming to kiss her, test the waters so-to-speak, but she'd already turned away. And it appeared they weren't alone anyhow.

The captain had come out of the cockpit and nodded to Westin, then asked Silvia if she needed anything else.

Westin stood, carefully, then thanked the captain and followed Silvia outside. She had a car already waiting for them. As they walked toward it, she called her brother, who answered.

"I just landed in Seattle," Silvia said into the phone. "How's Brighton?"

Westin heard Axel's deeper voice coming through the phone, but he couldn't make out the words.

"Really? Oh, that's good news, right?" She paused. "Well, I'm still coming. You can go home and get some sleep. But I'm so happy."

When she hung up, she turned to Westin, her smile wide. "Brighton is stabilized, and they think the baby might be fine after all. Brighton will have to be on bed rest, though. They're running more tests in the morning, but right now, they have hope."

"Wow, that's amazing."

"But I'm glad I came," Silvia said. "Brighton is like a sister to me, and I've . . ." She bit her lip. "I've been a pill the last couple of years. It will be good to apologize in person."

Westin nodded. Silvia Diaz was an impressive person.

"Oh, that's the car," she said, pointing to a red sedan. "The license plate matches my reservation."

He loved that her tone was lighter, as if a huge weight had been lifted, which it had.

As they settled into the back seat of the car, Silvia asked, "Do you want to be dropped off at my mom's so you can rest?"

The driver headed out of the airport, and within a few minutes, they were on a freeway.

Westin was currently focusing on keeping his breathing even. He hadn't taken anything for pain since what they'd given him at the clinic. "No, I'm coming with you, remember?"

She smirked. "That's pretty obvious. You're taking up more than your fair share of this back seat."

"My legs are long. Besides, you weren't complaining when you used me as a pillow earlier."

"That's because I don't talk in my sleep, which means I don't complain in my sleep, either."

Westin laughed at that, then groaned.

"What's wrong?" Silvia asked, scooting closer, her brown eyes full of concern.

"Uh, can you get the ibuprofen from my duffle?" He closed his eyes and slowly exhaled.

He listened to her rummage through the bag, then come up with the pill bottle. "Is this it? No prescription or anything?" she asked, handing it over.

He opened his eyes. "Four pills is prescription strength." He dumped four pills into his palm, then popped them into his mouth. He handed her the bottle for her to put away.

"You were written a prescription," she said. "I saw the doctor give it to you."

He winked. "We were in a hurry."

Silvia narrowed her eyes. "West, this isn't funny. You're in serious pain. Just a few hours ago, you were trampled by a bull."

"True story."

"You're going to my mom's to sleep," she said.

But Westin grabbed her hand. "No, darlin'. I didn't come to Seattle to get dumped off at a strange house."

"It's my mom's—"

Westin kissed her. It just happened. She was so close to him, and she smelled so sweet, and that worried look in her eyes was endearing.

She didn't move for a moment, then she kissed him back. Softly.

It was all over in mere seconds. Much too short.

"West," she whispered. "We need to talk... about us. But not right now."

"Sure thing." He drew her hand closer, onto his lap, his thumb moving over her wrist.

"And you can't touch me when we're around my brother," Silvia said in a low voice. "No hand-holding, no kissing, no sweet talk. And absolutely no moon eyes."

He had to smile at that. And the fact that she hadn't pulled her hand away.

"We need to be two feet apart, at least, or even more."

"When exactly are we going to have that talk?"

Silvia sighed. "Soon. After the hospital. Or maybe after we get some sleep."

Westin nodded. "I'm not going anywhere." Of course, that phrase had all kinds of connotations, and he meant each one. "But I do have good news."

"What's that?"

"I matched my dad's record."

Silvia's face transformed into a smile. "Are you serious? Just tonight—at the Prosper rodeo?"

He grinned. "The very one. The guys texted me on the plane. I won the bull riding over Knox Prosper, and broke the league record, which tops my dad's. My score was a perfect 100, which makes me one of three in the history of bull riding to achieve it."

"Wow." Silvia laughed. "I'm so happy for you." She leaned toward him, and then she did the sweetest thing. She kissed him. Briefly. When she drew away, she said, "Okay, that's the last time, but I'm just so happy for you."

"I didn't mind, darlin'," he said.

She sighed. "I'm sorry you're hurt, though. How can so many bad things now become good things?"

He squeezed her hand, and she squeezed back.

When the car pulled up to the hospital, true to her word, Silvia kept her distance. Westin had to respect her for her determination. It bothered him just a little that her brother was apparently still making some calls about their relationship. But if Silvia gave Westin the green light, then Axel would just have to learn to live with that.

They headed into the hospital and to the elevator that took them to the third floor—the maternity ward. A place Westin couldn't say he'd ever frequented. Silvia found the door they needed soon enough, and she said, "Wait here for a second."

"No problem." Westin leaned against the wall. Here in Seattle, his cowboy hat and boots seemed out of place.

The nurses glanced over at him more than once, and he nodded each time. One of them blushed. Oh. Well, maybe it was more than his hat and boots. He nearly laughed at his conceit. Must be more tired than he thought.

"Okay, you can come in," Silvia said, suddenly popping out of the door. She looked him up and down, as if realizing that a cowboy had truly followed her from Texas. "And by the way, Axel doesn't know you came."

"What?"

"He'll be fine. Remember, no touching."

"The animals at the zoo?"

"No, *me*." Her cheeks flushed. "And try to act . . . less *cowboy* around Axel. He's had a hard night." She blinked, as if realizing what she'd said. Westin's night hadn't been a piece of cake either. "Never mind."

"Don't worry, darlin', I'll be as well-behaved as a kid in church." He could tell she wasn't exactly convinced by the statement. Westin leaned close enough that he caught her sweet scent. "I think we should be more focused on your sister-in-law's health than the two cavemen in the room."

"Exactly," Silvia said, sounding relieved. "That's what I meant."

"Lead the way, darlin'."

"Don't call me darlin' around my brother."

"Yes, ma'am."

She sighed, then went back into the room. Westin followed.

The dark-haired woman in the bed was sleeping on her side, covers pulled up to her shoulder. Only a couple of lights were on, keeping the room dim.

The Axel he remembered wasn't the Axel now sitting on the other side of his wife's hospital bed. This man was hunched over, new lines about his face. He turned his head, saw Westin, and shot to his feet.

"Westin? What are you doing here?"

"He came with me," Silvia said.

Axel looked from Westin to Silvia, then back to Westin. Axel looked like he was trying to figure something out.

So Westin decided to help him out. "I was in the room when your mom called Silvia, and I offered to come with her."

Axel rubbed a hand over his face, then nodded. "Okay." He shot a glance at his sister, but she offered no additional information.

"Axel, you should go get some sleep," Silvia said. "You look like you've been dug up from a grave."

Axel gave a half-smile. "I feel like it, too, but I'm not leaving. You guys should go. To Mom's. I'll call you if there are any updates."

They all looked at Brighton, sleeping peacefully in the bed.

"Thanks for coming," Axel said in a soft voice.

Silvia smiled. "No problem. Cole Hunter came in handy."

Axel hugged Silvia goodbye, then he turned to Westin, who was still hovering by the door.

After a hesitation, Axel extended his hand.

Westin stepped forward and shook it. The handshake was brief, but in those few seconds, an accord was struck.

CHAPTER 27

"CAN WE HAVE THAT talk now?" Westin asked Silvia as they stood in the guest bedroom of her mom's condo.

Her mom was asleep, and Silvia had let herself in with her key. She'd led Westin through the dark rooms until they reached the guest bedroom, shut the door, and turned on a light.

Silvia should be exhausted, but her mind was keyed up. Brighton would be okay—she had to be. And Axel hadn't punched Westin out. That was major progress. Her brother was trusting her with this decision. Yet...

Gazing at Westin now, she knew she owed him the complete truth. No matter how much it might make things even more complicated.

He'd taken off his cowboy hat, and his dark blond hair was handsomely messy. But it was his eyes that pulled her in—wary, curious, and even vulnerable.

She hated that he was still in pain, too. No matter how he brushed it off, he carried himself gingerly. Even now, his breathing was more shallow than it should be. And she only wanted to take care of him. Make him rest, fix him food, fuss over his every ache and pain. Tell him to stop worrying about *her*.

She folded her arms, trying to buoy herself up. "Thanks for being patient with me, West."

His eyes flickered with something she couldn't read.

She'd never thought she'd have a cowboy over as a guest at her mom's place. It was surreal to have him standing here—in her space, in her life. "I've mostly gotten over what you and my brother did."

His brows furrowed. "Mostly?"

"It still stings," she said, "but I'm not mad about it anymore. If that makes sense?"

He gave a slow nod. "I never meant to hurt you."

"I know," she said. "That's one thing about you that I like. You put others first, and maybe that's why you were helping out my brother. It's just in your nature to help people."

His gaze remained steady on hers.

"And that's why I don't want to take advantage of you."

"How so?"

"By leading you on when I don't know what the future will bring."

"Silvia, don't say what I think you're going to say."

She smiled, but it was watery. "But it's what I want. And it's all I can promise."

Westin exhaled and looked away. After a long moment, he said, "I don't need a promise, darlin'." When he looked at her again, his eyes were hooded. "But if you tell me you just want to be friends, then that's what we'll be."

Silvia swallowed over the growing lump in her throat. "That's what I want. The past few weeks, I've been going through a lot of changes personally, dealing with my brother, coping with the reality that my panic attacks may never go away, and meeting you ... which has been ... wonderful." She hated that her voice cracked. "I'm healing, I'm figuring things out, I'm starting a new business, but I'm lost half the time. I hate to think that committing to anything with you will only wind up with things falling apart down the road because I've started out as such a mess. So . . . I really need you to just be a friend right now."

Westin's jaw ticked, but then he nodded. "Done."

She wanted to cry.

Instead, she whispered, "Thank you."

She left him in the guest room and found her way through the dark hallway to her own bedroom, which was next to her mom's. It was a long time before she fell asleep, knowing that she'd hurt Westin *again*, and knowing that this was also the best thing. Westin deserved a woman who could give her whole self to him, not just the broken parts. Would a friendship between them truly work? Or would things fade? Conversations turning to the occasional text, then melting into nothing at all?

When she awoke the following day, it was to the smell of food and conversation coming from the kitchen. Silvia grabbed her cell phone. It was almost noon, and there were two texts from Axel.

Brighton's tests all look good. The baby is fine. Brighton is being ordered to bed rest like they suggested before.

The second text read: *Talked to Mom. Brighton's going to stay at her place until baseball season is over.*

Silvia scrambled out of bed, elated. The baby was fine. Just some adjustments had to be made. She went into her bathroom and cleaned up quickly, then went out to investigate. She passed by the guest room. The door was open, and the bed stripped of the linens. Down the hall, the washing machine was going. Was her mom already washing Westin's sheets?

When she walked around the corner and into the kitchen, she stopped.

Westin was cooking at the stove, and her mom was sitting at the table, a cup of coffee in hand. Her mom was dressed in one of her favorite jogging suits, which meant she'd already gone for a walk around the small lake outside. Her dark hair, threaded with gray, was pulled into a ponytail, and she wore a ladies' Sharks baseball cap.

"Good morning, Silvia," her mom said, rising and hugging her.

"Hi, Mom." Over her mom's shoulder, she met Westin's gaze. He'd turned from the stove and winked. Then he turned back to whatever he was cooking.

"Your man here is making us brunch."

"He's not my—"

"Oh, he explained how you're just friends." Her mom drew away with a chuckle. "But if you change your mind, a man who cooks and does laundry is a catch."

Silvia scoffed. "Most men are functioning adults, Mom." She crossed to the stove. "What are you cooking?"

"I call it the Farr special," Westin said. "A little bit of everything."

It looked like he'd combined eggs, bacon, hash browns, peppers, and cheese all into one pan and was now cooking it together.

"Some hot sauce is all it needs now," he added.

"Smells good." She met his gaze, since it was still on her. He smelled like soap, and his hair was damp. "You're doing laundry, too?"

"Yes, ma'am," he said. "Getting the room ready for Brighton."

Her mom's phone rang, and it was one of her friends, because she began to chatter about Brighton's condition and how she was moving in with her.

But Silvia wasn't paying much attention, because Westin was looking at her with those mooning eyes again.

"Did you sleep okay?" he whispered.

"I did," she whispered back. "How are your ribs?"

"They've been better," he said. "But since you're not letting me touch you, that saves me a lot of physical effort there."

She held back a laugh. "Yet you're making breakfast and doing laundry? You should be sitting down, or even laying down."

"I'm fine, darlin'."

Silvia sighed and grasped his arm, pulling him toward the table. "Sit down, Westin Farr. I'm taking over now."

His lips twitched. "Yes, ma'am."

And she did. She finished cooking the last of the "Farr Special," set the table, poured juice into glasses, then found several types of hot sauces. She felt Westin's gaze on her the whole time while her mother chatted away.

"Mom, we're ready," Silvia said.

"I need to go," her mom said into the phone. "Let me know how everything goes with Mary's delivery." She hung up. "That was Bev. Her daughter is due any day."

"That's great, Mom," Silvia said. "What time will Axel and Brighton be here?"

"Soon," she said. "Axel said he was packing things for her at his place."

The washing machine stopped down the hall, and Westin began to rise from his chair. But Silvia placed a hand on his good shoulder. "Stay. I'll get it."

"You should eat," he said.

She held his gaze. "*You* should eat. I'll be right back."

His mouth quirked, and she held back a smile as she headed down the hall and switched the bedding into the dryer, then started it.

Just then, someone knocked on the front door. When she made it back down the hall, her mom was welcoming Brighton and Axel inside in a flurry of hugs and kisses. "Come in, come in. Westin made us brunch, and there's plenty for everyone."

Axel's gaze connected with Silvia's, but she couldn't read his expression. She stepped forward and gently hugged Brighton. She looked pale, but her smile was broad.

"Thanks for coming last night, even though I was asleep," Brighton said. "I can't believe you flew all the way home."

Silvia shrugged. "I was happy to. Now, come and eat. I'll grab you some plates."

Westin had already stood and greeted Brighton with a handshake. Brighton threw a significant look at Silvia, which she ignored.

While setting the other plates and dishing out more food, she mouthed to Westin: *Sit down.*

He did, and while they ate, her mom said, "We can move the television from my room into Brighton's. I don't watch it much, and I don't want her to get too bored."

"Oh, I have my laptop," Brighton said. "I'm not cutting back on my work hours."

Brighton used to be an airline stewardess, but after marrying Axel, she switched careers so she could travel to most of his games. She worked for a small advertising company that focused mostly on women's health products.

"I insist," her mom said. "Do you boys mind helping with that?"

"No problem," Axel said. "But I'm happy to buy a new TV."

"You're always so generous," Mom said, "but this arrangement will work out."

"So you're a bull rider?" Brighton asked Westin.

"Yes, ma'am."

Brighton looked intrigued. "What got you into that?"

"Grew up on a horse ranch in Oklahoma," he said. "And my dad was a bull rider, too."

Silvia blinked. She knew Westin was from Oklahoma and had assumed his family were some type of ranchers. But a *horse* ranch? She'd had no idea. He told everyone about his mom and sister, and then about the passing of his dad.

Just like the first time she'd met him, he didn't hold back his thoughts and emotions. He was an open book, and she should have never doubted his sincerity when he'd told her about his communications with Axel.

Silvia realized her brother was watching her watch Westin. She quickly changed her focus.

After the meal, Silvia said, "I'll clean up, and then get the bed put back together."

Westin was at her side in a moment. "I'll take care of the bed."

"And the TV," her mom chimed in.

"Of course," Westin said.

Silvia spun to face Westin. "No. You're sitting on the couch. I can help with the TV."

Everyone in the kitchen went silent. Maybe her voice had been sharper than she intended. She looked over at the surprised faces staring at her.

"Westin was trampled by a bull last night, and he has two broken ribs," she explained. If he wasn't going to tell anyone, then she was. "I was with him at the medical clinic when Mom called to tell me about Brighton."

"Goodness," her mom said. "You shouldn't be doing anything, young man. I agree with my daughter. Go rest on the couch."

"You were trampled?" Axel echoed.

Westin nodded, but didn't move.

"He also has a bum shoulder," Silvia added. "He's missing his MRI today because he came with me."

"It can be rescheduled, darlin'."

Silvia turned to him and said in a softer voice, "Okay, that's fine. But please don't move furniture around. Axel and I can take care of it." She paused. "Thanks for the offer, though."

Westin slid his gaze from her and looked at the others.

"I wouldn't recommend arguing with any of the Diaz women," Axel said simply.

"All right," Westin said. "I concede. Let me get my stuff out of the guest room."

Everyone watched him walk out of the kitchen, and before Silvia could explain anything else, Axel headed after Westin.

Silvia exhaled. *Was that good, or bad?*

"So..." Brighton raised her brows. "I guess I'm the one in the dark here, but who is that hot cowboy?"

"It's a long story."

Brighton grinned. "Well, I suddenly have a lot of time on my hands."

"Funny," Silvia said. "Now, keep it down. I want to go spy on them and hear what Axel is saying to my *friend*."

Brighton smirked.

Silvia headed down the hall. The door to the guest bedroom was shut. Interesting. And she could hear male voices coming from inside. She moved close and listened. Axel was asking Westin questions.

"So, you're just friends, huh?" Axel said, the doubt clear in his voice.

"That's what I said, sir."

"How does that work?"

"You never had a friend before?" Westin countered. "Phone calls, texts, showing up to important events—"

"I've had friends," Axel cut in, his voice tense. "But not a woman who I wasn't interested in dating."

"Oh, I'm interested," Westin said. "But like you said in the kitchen, it's better to listen to a Diaz woman rather than counter her."

"Okay, fair enough," Axel said. "So, you're friends. What are you getting out of it?"

"A friend," Westin deadpanned.

"There's got to be more."

No one spoke for a moment, then Westin said, "You're right. There's more. A lot more. I'm in love with your sister. But until she gives me the green light, we're staying friends."

Silvia's heart was about to explode. Was she hearing things? Did Westin just say . . .

"Does she know this?" Axel asked.

"She knows the friend part."

Silvia's pulse was thundering so loud that she almost didn't hear what her brother said next.

"And you're not going to tell her the other part?"

"I don't want to complicate things for her," Westin said. "She's dealing with a lot, and, well, I'm here as her friend. Nothing more. And I'd appreciate it if you'd stay out of our relationship when there are things that just concern the two of us."

Silvia waited for Axel to explode. He didn't. "You sound like Silvia, telling me to read that co-dependency book."

"Oh, I'm well familiar with that book," Westin said, amusement in his tone. "Kellie Prosper forced it upon me a few months after my dad's death. Told me I needed to cut my sister and mom some slack. Stop micromanaging their lives. Get back to riding bulls."

"Well, well."

Both men chuckled.

Silvia was stunned. What did this mean? They were buddies now? Bonding over their co-dependency?

"You're a good man, Farr," her brother said.

"It's an honor to hear that from you, Diaz," Westin said. "To be honest, I didn't know how this would all go down as far as me showing up in Seattle. But I couldn't let Silvia come alone."

"I understand," Axel said, his tone softer. "Thank you for that."

Whatever either of them was going to say next, Silvia could no longer stay in the hall. She turned the doorknob and walked into the room. Both men looked at her in surprise, but she was focused on only one man. The guy in a black t-shirt and faded jeans. The guy with the green eyes that seemed to stare into her soul and understand her every thought. "Can you give us a few minutes, Axe?" she told her brother without looking at him.

As soon as she heard the door click shut, Silvia continued toward Westin. She stopped in front of him and studied him for a moment. The soberness of his eyes, the scar on his jaw, the whisker scruff that had appeared overnight. He wasn't wearing his hat, or his boots, but he was still her cowboy.

Silvia took one more step forward and wrapped her arms about his neck. Westin didn't move, didn't react. His gaze searched her face, and there was that crease between his brows, as if he were worrying about her again. Maybe wondering if she'd lost her mind.

Silvia pushed up on her toes and moved her mouth close to his ear. "I changed my mind, Mr. Bull Rider. Friends isn't enough for me anymore. Do you want to change that status?"

His arms came around her then, and he drew her close. Then his lips were on hers. Soft, warm, familiar. She relaxed into him, trying to not put pressure in the area of his ribs, yet relishing in his strong body against hers. His hands moved up her back and tangled in her hair. He angled her head and took the kissing deeper.

"Is that a yes?" she whispered against his mouth.

"It's a hell yes," he rasped, then captured her in another long kiss.

The sounds in the other room faded away, and Silvia had no idea what everyone was thinking. Let them wonder and speculate. It would be obvious soon enough.

Westin's hands cradled her face, and he rested his forehead against hers. "What changed your mind, darlin'?"

"You," she whispered. "*You* changed my mind."

"In that case, we'd better make it official."

She drew back, eyeing him. "What do you mean?"

"I'm taking you to Oklahoma to meet my family."

CHAPTER 27

FLYING COACH DIDN'T EVEN compare to a private jet, but Westin's heart was floating above the highest cloud anyway.

Silvia Diaz was sleeping on his shoulder again, and he wouldn't have it any other way. He could get used to this—*was* used to this.

Two weeks had passed since the trip to Seattle, and the latest news was that Brighton was doing well and expected to carry her baby to full term. Axel had missed a couple of baseball games, but was now back on the road, with his mom fussing over his wife.

Westin and Silvia had headed back to Lost Creek together, where Westin stayed at Ryan's place at night, then bothered Silvia as much as possible during the day. Which mostly amounted to him helping her make barbeque sauce until she told him he had to stop helping and go rest. Which then resulted in an argument, followed by some makeup kissing. Or a lot of makeup kissing.

When Westin had suggested she come to Oklahoma with him, she hadn't turned him down, but she hadn't jumped at the chance, either. She said that maybe they should "date" for a while.

That "a while" turned out to be fourteen days, and here they were, heading toward the landing strip.

Westin's MRI results were also back, and he was hurt, but not injured. The doctor told him the rest to heal his ribs would also be beneficial to his shoulder.

Now, the airline captain's voice came onto the PA system. "We're about ten minutes to landing. Thanks for flying with us, folks. Sunny conditions and a mild wind are on the menu for the rest of the day."

Silvia lifted her head, her brown eyes bleary. "We're here?" She turned toward the window and lifted the shade.

The land below looked like a miniature farming community, and beyond that was the airport.

Westin took her hand and squeezed. "Home, sweet home."

She looked at him, then stifled a yawn. "How could you let me sleep? I told you not to."

"Because you're cute when you sleep." He leaned forward and kissed her softly.

She gave in for a half-second, then drew away. "I'll be wired all night now."

"Well, it's better than being grumpy around my family."

She swatted his knee. "You did not just say that."

He chuckled, and he leaned in for another kiss, which she gave.

"Ready to see Oklahoma?" he murmured as she drew away.

She slipped her hand into his and linked their fingers. "Ready."

For some reason, the heavens had decided to smile down upon Westin these past couple of weeks. No, he wasn't bull riding, but that was okay. That could wait. Right now, he was enjoying getting to know this beautiful, spunky woman at his side.

Cheryl was picking them up at the airport. She'd brought her son and their mom to the house so they could all meet Silvia.

Westin couldn't wait.

The plane seemed to take forever to reach its gate, and finally, they were off the plane, heading to the pickup zone.

As soon as he saw Cheryl, with her blonde hair and green eyes, he drew her into a soft hug. His ribs were much better, but he was still supposed to be careful.

"Hug me next, Uncle West," a little voice said.

Westin crouched and pulled three-year-old Jeppsen into his arms.

"You're squishing me!" Jeppsen said with a giggle. He was a mini-me of his dark-haired dad, complete with brown eyes.

Cheryl's husband had a big case this week, so he hadn't been able to make the trip.

Westin released his nephew, then straightened. "Cheryl and Jeppsen, I'd like you to meet Silvia Diaz."

"You're not very tall," Jeppsen declared.

Everyone laughed. Cheryl was five-ten, and Jeppsen's dad was over six feet.

"Then I guess we should be friends," Silvia said, not missing a beat.

Jeppsen beamed, his brown eyes bright. "Do you like trucks?"

Silvia glanced at Westin, then said, "I love trucks."

"My daddy has a blue one," Jeppsen announced. "He says I'm too little to drive it yet. Maybe next year."

"Next year, huh?" Silvia said.

The two of them chattered all the way to the parking lot, where Jeppsen pouted when he didn't get to sit by Silvia, but Westin reminded him, "The ladies sit up front. Us gentlemen sit in the back."

Jeppsen then proudly showed off how he could buckle himself into his booster seat.

It was good to listen to Cheryl and Silvia talk. So far, so good. Cheryl asked all kinds of questions about Silvia's barbeque sauce, and Westin was content to listen.

Silvia was working out of Lost Creek, but would she stay there? Would she be drawn back to Seattle once she became an aunt? Or . . . Westin gazed out the window as they passed a farm. Would she ever consider Oklahoma?

When they arrived at the family ranch, his mom was out front in the flower bed, weeding. She was wearing a medical boot on her foot, and her knee scooter was nearby.

"That stubborn woman," Westin muttered.

"Who's stubborn?" Jeppsen asked. "Grandma?"

"No one's stubborn," Cheryl said, shooting Westin a warning look in the rearview mirror.

"Your mom's right," Westin said. "No one's stubborn."

Cheryl parked her SUV, and as soon as she did, Jeppsen was out of his booster seat like Houdini. When she opened the back door, she said, "I told you to wait until I help you."

"I can do it myself!" Jeppsen declared.

Westin chuckled; he couldn't hold it back.

"Not helping," Cheryl told him.

Westin only smiled and climbed out, meeting Silvia.

His mom had stopped pulling weeds, and she was now hobbling over to the knee scooter. He grasped Silvia's hand and led her to his mom while Cheryl continued to deal with Jeppsen.

"Wow, this place is beautiful," Silvia said, her hand tightening on his.

Westin nodded. The ranch spread out before them, with the two-story white house and its wraparound porch at the forefront. Acres spread on each side, horse property, beneath a bright blue sky. To the side of the house, back a couple of hundred feet, was the main barn, and beyond that, fenced-in grazing pastures.

"Mom, this is Silvia Diaz."

She smiled, her blonde hair with its whiter streaks blowing in the light wind. "Nice to meet you, Silvia."

"You, too, Mrs. Farr," Silvia said, holding out her hand. "This is a beautiful place."

His mom brushed her hands on her jeans. "Oh, my hands are dirty. Welcome to the ranch. I was just getting a few things weeded."

"Mom, you're not supposed to be doing labor," West said, stepping forward to kiss her cheek.

"Two peas in a pod, I'd say," Cheryl said, joining them. "Both injured, but neither are taking it easy."

"How is your ankle?" Silvia asked his mom.

"Better every day," his mom said. "Come on in. We've got food ready. All of Westin's favorites."

"Mom, you shouldn't have," he protested. "Again, you're supposed to be recovering."

His mom only winked and led the way, expertly maneuvering her scooter ahead of them.

Silvia squeezed his hand and looked up at him. "What are your favorite foods, West?"

"I guess we'll find out."

His mom must have been fixing food all day, because there were several covered dishes on the counter and a crockpot of stew.

Cheryl told Jeppsen to sit at the table, then she uncovered the prepared dishes and started to bring them to the table.

"I can do that," Westin said, lifting a salad bowl.

"You sit down," Silvia said at the same time Cheryl did.

They looked at each other and laughed.

"I think I can carry a salad bowl," Westin said, but Silvia was giving him her best warning look. So he set the salad bowl on the table and took a seat.

"You didn't have to do all this, Mom," Westin said.

There were mashed potatoes, green salad, cornbread, fresh fruit, and steak stew.

His mom only smiled and extended her hand to him, and he took it. Then he grasped Silvia's hand, too.

"Can I say grace?" Jeppsen popped up, kneeling in his chair so that he looked like a tall little man at the other end of the table.

"Of course, hon," Cheryl said.

Westin's lips twitched as little Jeppsen prayed over the food, the horses, Silvia's visit—he called her Sivvy—his daddy's meetings, and that his mom wouldn't break any more nails. When he finished, everyone was holding back laughter.

"Did you break a nail this morning, sis?" Westin asked.

She smirked. "I did. And thank you, Jeppsen, for the beautiful prayer."

As they started to eat, Silvia said, "This is delicious, thank you so much, Mrs. Farr."

"You're welcome, dear," his mom said.

Westin stayed quiet for the most part as the women talked. His mom seemed to like Silvia, and asked her plenty of questions.

And Silvia asked questions back.

Westin couldn't think of any scenario where it would have gone better.

"You must be a special woman," his mom said.

Westin paused mid-bite. Where was she going with this?

"Not much could come between Westin and his bull riding," she continued.

"Only his horses," Cheryl added with a laugh. "When

Westin is home, he eats, then spends all his time out on the ranch. Driving our ranch manager, Dustin, crazy with all his suggestions."

Westin lowered his fork. "I'm not that bad. Besides, the last time I was here, he hadn't even noticed a crack in the feeding trough."

"So you say," his mom said. "Dustin has a different story."

Westin scoffed.

"Anyway," his mom continued. "After we eat, don't worry about cleanup. I'll take care of that. You and Westin can go ride about the property before the sun sets."

"Ride?" Silvia's forehead creased. "You mean on a *horse?*"

His mom's brows popped up. "Of course."

"Oh, I don't ride horses," Silvia said. "I don't even care for them that much. I mean, they're beautiful animals. From a distance."

No one at the table spoke. Then his sister and mom's gazes shifted to him. Both of them were silently asking the same question. *How in the world are you dating a woman who hates horses?*

Westin reached for his ice water and took a long, deep swallow. Then he set the glass down slowly. "I'm not allowed on a horse for a few more weeks, anyway."

"Well, Silvia," his mom said, her tone about an octave higher. "We have plenty of horses you can view from a distance."

From the corner of his eye, he could tell that his sister was trying not to crack up.

"I think we'll take you up on your offer, Mom," he said. "I'll show Silvia around the ranch, but we'll just wave to the horses."

Cheryl snorted, then covered it up by pretending she had to cough.

"We should clean up first," Silvia countered.

He stood and reached for her hand. "The sun will be down in less than an hour, so we need to go now unless you want to wait until tomorrow."

Silvia looked about the table, and when his mom and sister nodded at her, she said, "All right."

They walked out onto the front porch, and Westin kept her hand in his. The sky had already warmed to peach as the sun inched toward the western horizon.

"Did I screw up in there?" Silvia asked as they walked around the house.

"Nah. You just surprised the womenfolk in my family, that's all."

"Because of the horse thing?"

He slowed his step and pulled her to a stop.

"Let me teach you how to ride," he said, slipping his hands about her waist. He pressed a kiss against her jaw.

"Are you trying to butter me up?"

"Is it working, darlin'?"

She trailed her hands up his arms and over his biceps, then stopped at his shoulders. "A little."

He chuckled. "Come on, I want you to meet Madeline. She's the sweetest mare you'll ever meet."

Frankly, he was surprised Silvia didn't put up more of a fuss as they walked into the barn. He smiled as she marveled at the number of horses they kept inside.

"We have a dozen more in the pasture right now."

"So many, for what?"

"Breeding, mostly," he said. "Then we sell them to other ranchers, and the thoroughbreds are sold for racing."

"Like horse racing?"

Westin tried not to laugh. "Yes, ma'am."

She smirked. "Okay, who's this Madeline?"

Westin led her to the farthest stall, where the bay stood. Her dark red coat was lustrous in the light of the sunset shining through the open barn doors. "First, you need to introduce yourself to a horse."

"Oh, really?" Silvia said.

Westin nodded. "Go ahead, darlin'."

Silvia turned to the bay. "Hello, Madeline, I'm Silvia Diaz."

The horse seemed to nod.

"Does she understand me?" Silvia asked.

Westin only smiled. "Now, hold out your hand so she can smell you."

The horse nudged Silvia's hand when she held it out. "It tickles," she said with a laugh.

"Now, tell her you're going to stroke her," he said.

Tentatively at first, Silvia ran her fingers along the horse's coat. Then she used her whole hand. "I didn't realize how smooth and silky her coat was." Silvia continued to stroke, her eyes not leaving the bay.

"If you ask if you can ride her, very politely, then she'll say yes."

Silvia snapped her gaze to him. "I'm not riding her."

"Yes, you are."

She blinked. "West."

"We can walk around the barn, and I'll hold the reins the whole time."

Silvia gazed at him for a moment, as if weighing the risks in her mind. "Okay. One lap around the barn."

Westin almost cheered. Instead, he said, "All right, time to learn about tack."

Silvia was on the horse fifteen minutes later, after he'd

taught her about the tack. Atop the horse, Silvia's expression was a mixture of horror and delight, and her grip on the bridle made her knuckles turn white.

"Relax, darlin'," Westin said. "Madeline is going to walk easy. You'll be fine. I promise." He met her gaze, and he could see the vulnerability in her brown eyes, but there was also trust.

"Ready?" he continued. "We're heading outside now."

True to his word, he led her around the barn, only once. And if Westin was being honest, Silvia looked dang fine on a horse, her dark hair tumbling about her shoulders as the sky behind her deepened to violet.

"One more time," she said as they neared the barn doors.

Westin grinned. "Here we go." He led her around the barn again, but this time he said, "You hold the reins."

She shook her head, but he pressed, "I'll still be right here, and Madeline wouldn't dare disobey her new friend."

"All right," Silvia said in a small voice, then she did indeed grasp the reins from him.

Soon, Silvia was riding the horse on her own, and once they reached the barn doors the second time, she said, "How do we turn?"

"Tug to the left."

Silvia did. "It worked!"

Westin was still smiling by the time Silvia reined the horse to a stop. He instructed her how to dismount. When she was on the ground, she turned toward him. "I can't believe I did it!"

"I'm proud of you, darlin'." He leaned down and brushed his lips against hers. "Now, let's get her back into her stall and ready for the night."

Silvia seemed to be soaking in everything he was showing her, and she was a fast learner. He introduced her to the other horses, and she stroked each one. As the moments passed, he could feel her ease growing. That was a good thing.

By the time they left the barn and he shut the doors, the sun had set, and the violet sky was now a deeper blue.

Stars began to peek through the darkened sky.

Silvia slipped her hand into his, and he linked their fingers.

"This place is so beautiful, West," she said. "And peaceful. Oh, is that where the other horses are?" She pointed to the far pasture.

"Sure is."

She continued to the fence, then leaned against it. Westin wrapped both of his arms about her from behind, then rested his chin on the top of her head.

"Why doesn't your mom live here?"

He'd told Silvia about his mom staying at his sister's place a lot, even before her ankle surgery. "I think home reminds her too much of my dad."

"And your sister doesn't want to live here, either?"

"Her husband's commute would cut into family time too much," he said. "He has frequent court dates."

Silvia nodded, then leaned more fully against him. "And you chose bull riding?"

"For now," he said. "My sister and mom insisted I finish out my career in bull riding. The ranch will always be here for me. But since I matched my dad's record, I'm thinking that retiring from bull riding might be in order sooner than later."

Silvia turned in his arms, facing him. The exterior lights from the barn and the rising moon gave him enough light to see her. "And this is what you want? To live here and run the ranch?"

"It is," he said in a soft voice. "Or it was. Until recently. I've been considering other options."

Silvia bit her lip. "Like what?"

"Like hanging out wherever you're running your business."

Her eyes widened, then a small smile crept onto her face. "I'm making barbeque sauce, West. That can be done anywhere."

"It can?" he asked, partly teasing, partly not.

"According to the distributor, it doesn't matter where I ship from," she said. "I asked him yesterday."

He studied her, looking for the meaning of what she was saying. He rested his hands on her hips and pulled her against him. "Think you can ship from a ranch in Oklahoma?"

She slipped her hands around his waist, and his heart skipped a beat. "Maybe if I had the right cowboy helping me."

"I might know someone," he said with a wink.

She laughed softly, then she drew back a few inches. "I have a confession."

Good or bad, he wanted to hear it. "You'd better tell me, then."

"I heard you talking to Axel in Seattle," she said.

Westin raised his brows. This, he hadn't expected. Did he even remember what exactly they'd talked about? And then he did remember. "Oh. That."

"Is it true?"

"That I'm in love with you? Yes, it's true."

"And when were you going to tell me?"

Westin could have been knocked over by a feather if one had headed his way. "Is now a good time?"

Silvia's smile was coy. "Yes."

He lifted a hand to her cheek, his thumb making a slow caress along her skin. "Silvia Diaz, I'm in love with you."

She released his waist and looped her arms about his neck, bringing them flush together. "That's good to hear, because I'm in love with you, too, Westin Farr."

Was it possible for his heart to take flight and soar straight up to the moon?

He wanted to give her a kiss that she'd never forget, but first he had a question. "Would you ever consider coming to Oklahoma, darlin'?"

Her smile made his breath halt. "I would."

"How soon? Because I was thinking the sooner, the better."

She laughed. "Do you have an incentive for me, or something? I mean, I'd have to relocate, change everything, and that's a lot to ask."

Westin's smile spread. "I agree, darlin', it is a lot. Would a diamond ring and a promise of forever be enough of an incentive?"

Silvia's beautiful eyes widened. "You'd better not be fooling around, Westin Farr."

"I'm dead serious, Silvia Diaz. Cross my heart."

"Well, then . . ." She tightened her arms about his neck, bringing her sweet self even closer. "I guess I'm coming to Oklahoma."

So, Westin gave her that unforgettable kiss, one that signified the beginning of their forever. One that promised tomorrow would be another beautiful day with this woman. One that proved to him that two hearts could heal when joined.

Silvia's Guacamole

3 avocados, ripened
1/2 small onion, finely diced (Silvia uses white onion)
2 Roma tomatoes, diced
2 tbsp fresh cilantro, chopped
1 jalapeno pepper, seeds removed and finely diced (optional)
Garlic salt, to taste preference
1–2 limes, juiced (Silvia uses 2 limes)
1/2 tsp sea salt

Instructions: Slice the avocados in half, remove the pit and skin, and place in a mixing bowl.

Mash the avocado with a fork and make it as chunky or smooth as you'd like.

Add the remaining ingredients and stir together.

Silvia's Barbeque Sauce

2 cups ketchup (you can use refined sugar-free, if needed)
½ cup coconut sugar (or ½ cup brown sugar gives it a heavier molasses flavor)
½ cup apple cider vinegar
2 tsp each: Dijon mustard and Worcestershire sauce
1 tsp each: garlic powder, onion powder, and chili powder (you can also use Season-All)
6 drops liquid smoke

Other optional add-ins: Lemon Juice (1 tbsp) or a splash of hot sauce

Instructions: Whisk the ingredients in a small pan over medium-high heat. Bring the pot to a boil, then reduce the heat to medium-low and simmer for 10 minutes, stirring occasionally. Remove the pan from the heat and allow the barbeque sauce to cool before using or storing it.

Want more Lost Creek Rodeo?
Visit our series page on Amazon!

Interested in Knox Prosper's story?
Check out *Not Over You*, or the entire
Prosperity Ranch series!

Heather B. Moore is a four-time *USA Today* bestselling author. She writes historical thrillers under the pen name H.B. Moore; her latest thrillers include *The Killing Curse* and *Breaking Jess*. Under the name Heather B. Moore, she writes romance and women's fiction. Her newest releases include the historical novels *The Paper Daughters of Chinatown* and *Deborah: Prophetess of God*. She's also one of the coauthors of the *USA Today* bestselling series: A Timeless Romance Anthology. Heather writes speculative fiction under the pen name Jane Redd; releases include the Solstice series and *Mistress Grim*. Heather is represented by Dystel, Goderich & Bourret.

For book updates, sign up for Heather's email list:
hbmoore.com/contact
Website: HBMoore.com
Facebook: Fans of Heather B. Moore
Blog: MyWritersLair.blogspot.com
Instagram: @authorhbmoore
Pinterest: HeatherBMoore
Twitter: @HeatherBMoore

www.ingramcontent.com/pod-product-compliance
Lightning Source LLC
LaVergne TN
LVHW021807060526
838201LV00058B/3276